Dance is the Secret Event

by Melisa Torres

Illustrated by Daniel Ramos

ISBN: 978-1-48358-453-9

ISBN: 978-1-48358-454-6

For my Dad. Thank you for attending every State Meet, wearing all my photo pins at once, and taking tons of pictures.

I know it wasn't softball, but I think we had a good run.

– Mel

Chapter 1

Battements in Dance

"Ladies, you have a new dance coach today," James tells us. I'm stretching on the floor with my Level 3 teammates. We are listening to our coach, James, explain what we are going to be working on today.

"Why do we even need dance?" Trista asks.

"Because dance can be the difference between polished versus sloppy gymnastics. The difference between winning and losing," he says.

If James says dance is how you win, then I am going pay attention in dance class. I want to place in the All-Around at our State Meet. I really think I can do it. I placed in the All-Around at the last three meets of the season. I wonder if State will be harder than a regular meet?

"State Meet isn't just a regular meet," James continues, reading my mind. "The competitors are going to be top notch and we need to step up our game. Cleaning up our form and dance is a place to do that. So, today you are going to start with the dance rotation. Go get your tights on and head upstairs," he orders.

We get up out of our splits and go into the lobby where our bags are in the cubbies along the wall. I get to my cubby first and pull out my gym bag. I rummage through and find my tights and ballet slippers. I sit down to put on my tights over my leotard as I listen to my teammates talk.

"Do you have the wolf Beanie Boo?" Alexis asks Marissa.

"I have one that's a Huskie, not a wolf. His name is Slush, is that the one you're thinking of?" Marissa asks.

"I think so, gray and white, Drew has it. It's so cute, that's my favorite one," Alexis says.

"Is there a bunny Beanie Boo?" Savannah asks.

Since I could care less about Beanie Boos I stand up and finish pulling my tights on. Then I go to the stairs and up to the dance area. As much as I love my teammates, sometimes their chatter seems childish to me. After all, I am ten years old, two years older than most of them. I wish I could fit in more and care about Beanie Boos, but I don't.

I stand in the doorway of the dance studio and look at my reflection in the floor to ceiling dance room mirrors. I don't really look like a gymnast because I have on pink tights and black ballet slippers. But I don't look like a dancer either because my pink tights are pulled over my leotard. We do this so we can get back to our gymnastics workout faster after our ballet rotation.

3

I walk to the middle of the room. There are mirrors and ballet barres on three walls and a window to the training area on the far left wall.

What would it be like to be a real dancer? I think as a pull my hair up from a pony tail into a tucked under half pony tail, which, with my crazy hair, looks like a bun. I have bright red hair with tiny curls that spring up everywhere. No amount of gel, spray, frizz ease, or cream will put my curls down.

I can hear my teammates running up the stairs like a herd of elephants. For a bunch of petite little third graders, they sure do make a lot of noise.

"Is Megan still ignoring you at school?" I hear Trista ask Savannah as they stumble through the doorway.

"Yes, but I know she doesn't like to," Savannah answers.

"Oh, hey Paige, you got up here fast," Trista says. Not really, they were just slow getting on their tights because they were all busy talking.

I shrug in response as they start doing gymnastics poses in front of the mirrors.

Alexis runs over to the viewing window on the left wall, "Look at the boys' team tumble, they're so sloppy," she says. This makes all the girls run over and look out the window.

"I can't believe Tyler lets them throw back tucks out of that garbage," Trista comments.

"Hello girls," we hear. We all turn to see our new ballet teacher. She is the tallest thinnest woman I have ever seen. She is wearing pink tights with a black leotard over them and a transparent black flowing skirt around her waist. She makes our tights over our leotards look awkward. Her hair is in a perfect dark blond bun and she floats gracefully to the front of the room.

"I am your new Madame." *Our what?* James said we had a new dance teacher, but I assumed she would be a coach like our past dance teachers. This lady is not a gymnastics coach. Most gymnastics coaches used to be gymnasts. They are short and muscular, not tall and willowy. "I am from the Salt Lake City Ballet Company and I will be teaching you traditional ballet." *Isn't that what we have been doing?*

"Kathryn hired me to prepare you for the State Meet you have coming up. Take your place at the barre and we will start with tendus."

The rest of the team is standing stunned by the window. Her announcement to begin broke the trance and the girls start being their lively selves again. Trista cartwheels over to the other side of the room while Savannah skips next to her, Marissa runs over to the barre at the back of the room, and Alexis sashays over to Marissa's barre. I look around and the only barre left is the one by the window, so I walk over to it and stand next to the barre all by myself.

Chapter 2

Handstand Pirouette on Floor

We are in place at the barres, but there is still a lot of talking going on. I seem to be the only one who notices the appalled expression of our new teacher.

The ballet madame stands there staring at us quietly with a stern expression. Finally, my teammates stop talking and notice she is waiting for us.

"Are you girls done wasting your time?" she asks us a bit snooty. We have the good sense to nod. I feel embarrassed for my teammates and I feel bad for this new teacher. She's obviously used to teaching at a formal establishment. Is ballet more intense than gymnastics? I wonder what a real studio is like.

"Do you know why I am here?" She asks.

We are silent, not sure whether we're supposed to answer the question or not. "I am here," she continues, "because Kathryn feels that all her teams are lacking grace and quality to their performances. James has informed me you are in the middle of your competition season and we only have two weeks to see improvement." She looks at us and we look at her. I have never seen my team so quiet.

"Correct dance will change your performances in a very subtle way. Judges and audiences will see it, they will feel it, they will enjoy your performance," she explains.

She keeps saying the word performance. I don't think of our routines as a performance, or us as performers. I think of us as athletes doing a sport.

"Are you girls ready to learn to dance?" We nod silently. "Good, then let's start with tendus. Fifth position." I settle into my spot and raise my arm to the side for our tendus.

"Hmm. Do you girls not know fifth position for the arms?" she asks.

None of us answer her question because she is a little scary and the last questions she answered for herself anyway.

But the silence stretches and finally Alexis speaks up.

"We know," Alexis answers, "we usually keep our arms in second position for most of our drills because we get confused."

"Confused," she says, pressing her lips together. "I see. Well, let's do it how you are used to and we can make changes from there."

She has us do tendus and then battements. I enjoy the foot work and the music and feeling my body stretching out and moving through the positions. We end each set in relevé and turn to do the other side. As I'm doing the battements on my second side I can see my teammates. Marissa looks like a solider, stiffly going through her movements and Alexis looks like a limp noddle and I can tell neither of them are enjoying themselves.

I peek over to Savannah and Trista and they are even worse. They are whispering and giggling to each other. I'm afraid to look back and see Madame's expression. We turn back to the other side so I am facing front again to start our passés. I look at our poor teacher. Even though her posture is perfect, her neck is long, and her head is held high, I can see she looks overwhelmed. This makes me giggle, *are we that awful?* Maybe we are compared to her dancers, but can they do a back handspring? I bet not.

"Alright girls, let's move to the center and do some pirouettes."

"Really? Best dance class ever!" Trista bounces to the center of the room and kicks up to a handstand and starts trying to walk on her hands in a circle. She falls pretty fast because handstand pirouettes are hard to do.

I sneak another look at our new teacher and she seems to be a combination of shocked and impressed.

I take pity on her *and* Trista. "Trista, in dance, a pirouette is what gymnasts call a full turn."

"Oh," she says, bummed as she picks herself off the ground.

"In gymnastics," I say, turning to the Madame, "we call walking on our hands in a circle a pirouette."

The madame gives me a weak smile and says, "Thank you . . .?"

"Paige," I supply.

"Thank you, Paige, for explaining things to me. I can see this is going to be a new challenge for me. You girls do a lot of the same things as dancers, but approach them differently."

"What do you mean?" Marissa asks curiously.

"Well," she begins, "when you girls tendu, you immediately tighten your leg muscles, you bunch them up. A dancer extends her muscles, makes them longer," she explains.

I look down at my legs and try a tendu both ways, one with a quick squeeze and one trying to extend my leg out. They *are* different.

"Very nice Paige," she comments and I look over to see everyone staring at me.

"Let's do more tendus, practicing it right here how Paige is doing it. Try it both ways so you can feel the difference."

"Seriously? Instead of turns?" Trista moans.

"Yes, you girls need to understand the difference. Badly," she replies.

"Way to ruin the fun Paige," Trista mumbles under her breath.

Chapter 3

Glide on Bars

After dance we file down the stairs into the lobby.

We head to our cubbies to take off our tights and ballet

slippers and put our workout shorts over our leotards for the rest of our gymnastics practice.

"That was so boring," Trista complains.

"Yeah," Marissa agrees, "I would rather be doing gymnastics. But every other week is no big deal."

"I'm surprised we're even doing dance in the middle of season, we have our routines to work on," Trista continues.

"But aren't we ready?" asks Marissa. "I mean, we did fine last meet, not much left to work on," Marissa reasons.

"For you maybe," Trista mumbles under her breath.

Then Savannah changes the subject and starts talking about her friends at school. I tune them out as I watch the ballet teacher, or Madame, talking to James. Based on his expression, he is not getting good news about our dance rotation. We are a bit of a disaster. We don't really know the arm positions, we only do leaps on our good side, and we know inside turns but not outside turns. On top of all that she was frustrated that we hide our necks, have stressed out fingers, and stick our bums out too far. Yeah, I'm sure the report to James is not good.

James finishes his conversation with the ballet teacher and walks over to us. "Ladies, get a drink and meet me at bars."

We do as he says and he is waiting for us at bars. "Well, ladies, apparently you have a long way to go in dance. Madame says Paige showed her there is hope and has requested to work with you every workout until State Meet."

"Twice a week! Every workout!?" Trista screeches.

"Yes, it's what will set you guys apart at State on beam and floor. Unlike the optional teams, we don't have much time."

"Great. Thanks Paige," Trista says sarcastically.

"What did I do?" I ask.

"You showed her we have hope," she sulks. This makes James and me laugh, which makes Trista sulk even more.

"Okay, ladies, let's focus on bars. Start with three sets of three glides." We get to work on bars, and thankfully the dance fiasco is forgotten.

"Don't be so grumpy with Paige," I hear Savannah defend me as she and Trista climb into Savannah's mom's car. "She just likes dance, kind of how you like floor," I hear Savannah say as she shuts the car door. This makes me smile to myself. Savannah is a really cute kid. She's only in second grade, the rest of the girls are in third grade and I am in fifth. Sometimes I forget there is an age difference. But lately, like today in dance class, I can tell. Then again, Savannah surprises me with something so mature, like understanding me and defending me to Trista.

I let out a sigh and see my breath cloud up in front of me. It's getting cold these late fall days in Snowcap Canyon. We live in Utah surrounded by massive mountains. My house is way up at the top of one of the mountains. My guess is that it will be snowing by the end of the month; by State Meet.

The cold is starting to get to me since I'm only wearing a leotard, gymnastics shorts, and a sweatshirt. I wonder if I should be waiting outside or if I should go back in the gym and wait for my mom there. Where is my mom anyway? Recently she's been distracted, forgetful, and late for things. Then I see her car turning into the parking lot and driving to the front door.

I open the door when she pulls up and she immediately starts apologizing. "Sorry! So sorry pumpkin."

"It's okay," I assure her as I climb in. "It's getting cold as soon as the sun goes down," I comment.

"Winter is close," she agrees, "where are your sweat pants?" she asks, all worried and mom-like.

"I just wore the sweatshirt," I answer buckling up.

She frowns and I can tell she is trying to think back to when she dropped me off and why she didn't notice I wasn't wearing pants over my shorts.

"We got a new ballet teacher today," I share, trying to get her mind off worrying about my clothing.

"Yeah? Why?" she asks.

"Katie said we need a real ballet teacher instead of gymnastics coaches. She said that she's tired of all her teams looking sloppy and that we need to learn it right as soon as possible," I explain. "The Optional Teams don't start competing until January so they have more time to get better than we do. But Katie said to start us with the new dance teacher anyway."

"What's she like?" my mom asks.

"Oh mom, she's beautiful," I gush. "And scary and interesting," I add.

My mom glances back at me through the rear view mirror. "How was she scary?"

"Not scary, just stern, I guess. She teaches real ballet, like, at a ballet company downtown. And up until now I thought we were doing real ballet, now I see we weren't," I explain.

My mom chuckles, "Then what were you doing?"

"Based on the expression on her face today, we were doing a sloppy job of imitating ballet."

"Oh pumpkin, you guys are just kids, I'm sure she expected as much," she laughs

"Seriously mom, you should have seen her face," I say and start giggling. "I think she's never been in a room with gymnasts before and we are kind of, well, kind of bouncy and loud," I say laughing harder.

My mom joins me with a little laugh, "Maybe this will be good. You guys can teach her to let loose a little, and she can teach you to take the dance part of your training more seriously."

I'm silent for a moment. That is exactly right. It seems like Madame whatever-her-name-was needed to laugh more and my team, well, we definitely need to respect dance more.

"How many weeks until State?" My mom asks breaking the silence.

"Two," I say and I can hardly wait. I'm ready and I really think I can place in the top ten in the All-Around.

"What does James say?" My mom asks referring to my coach.

"That we're ready and it's time to clean up our skills and our dance."

"Do you feel ready?" she asks, looking again in the mirror.

"Yeah," I say, "beam doesn't bother me like it does the other girls and bars is no big deal. I'm thinking I can maybe place in the All-Around," I admit.

Chapter 4

Front Mil Circle on Bars

I am never going to place in the All-Around.

"Red, what's going on over there?" James yells
from the set of uneven bars to me at the quad bars. I
just fell on my mil circle for the third time. And honestly,
I'm not sure what's going on. I look over at him and
shrug. "Your turn with me anyway, try it again here,"
he says. During the bars rotation James works with us
one at a time on the competition set of bars while the

rest of us practice on a set of four low bars called the quad bars.

"Want to tell me why you keep stopping your wrists?" he asks.

"I wasn't stopping my wrists," I defend myself.

His gray eyes look at me for a second and I feel bad I just talked back to him, but now I don't know what to say. Thankfully he tries again, "Want to tell me what you were thinking about then?"

"You told us to pretend it was a meet, and I did, and that's what happened," I sulk.

This makes James throw his head back and laugh. "You have such a good imagination that you were nervous over there?"

"Well, yeah. Don't laugh, it was your idea!"

"Okay, okay, you're right," he tries to hide his smile and takes a breath. "Paige, you have competed four meets this season and managed to stay on bars all season, why would you be nervous now, even if you're pretending?"

"I dunno," I say lamely.

Out of the corner of his eye he sees Alexis do a sloppy front hip circle, "Keep those legs straight, Lex." Then he looks back at me, waiting for a real answer.

"It's State," I say, as if this explains everything. "And well, I want – ," I pause not saying I want to win, or that I think I can place in the All-Around. I'm a little embarrassed that this is my goal because it means beating my teammates. "I want to do really well," I finish.

"Of course you want to do well. But you're not going to do well working yourself up into a tizzy. You have the makings of a great bar worker, you're clean and you can swing." I nod, but I'm not sure what to say back. "Do a routine and let's see what the problem is," he instructs.

I start with my glide, pull over, and front hip circle. I can do all of these skills easily. Then I do the shoot through with no problem and lift up my leg for the mil circle. I swing forward but as I am coming around the bar to finish my body stops. I swing backwards in a basket swing instead of ending back at the top of the bar where I started.

"Let's stop here," James says as I swing myself back up to where I should have ended my mil circle. "Do you think about shifting your wrists or do you just do it?" he asks.

"I just do it," I answer.

"And somehow today, you have stopped doing it and you can't make your mil circle around?" he asks and I nod. "Alright, so your mind has interfered and now you need to be more aware of how to complete the skill," he thinks out loud. "Trista!" he yells over to the quad bars, "I'm sending Paige over. Show her how to do the wrist drills for mil circles," he yells.

"Okay, Coach," she says. Somewhere along the way some of us have started calling James 'Coach.' It's unusual in gymnastics, but Alexis started it because her brothers call their baseball coaches 'Coach.'

I walk over to Trista, curious about this drill I never knew about. "Marissa, your turn!" James yells. Marissa jumps down from her spot next to Trista and runs over to James' bar.

"Wrist drills, huh?" Trista says as I walk up. I nod. "All you do is stand here and put your hands on the bar in a front grip with straight arms. Practice rotating them up, like this," she says, showing me a few times. "The idea is that when you are coming around in the mil circle you know how to shift your wrists instead of leaving them behind," she explains.

I put my hands on the bar in a front grip position and practice rotating my hands from the under the bar to the side. I practice this a few times and I notice Trista is staring at me.

"What?" I say.

"All those great bar routines and you never knew this before?" she asks.

"I just didn't think about it, I guess," I admit.

"Man, I think about everything on bars and I still can't get it," she shares. I drop my arms to my sides and frown.

"You will Trista. Not every event is going to be easy. We all have an event we hate," I say, trying to make her feel better.

"What about Savannah? What's hard for her?" she asks with a pout.

This makes me laugh, "I don't know yet. Maybe when she gets to Level 10 it will get hard," I say and we quietly giggle.

"Okay ladies, time for dance," James yells, interrupting our fun. This gets a loud groan from Trista.

"Really James? We have to do dance every practice? Every other week was bad enough," she whines.

"Until Julia says you look like dancers, it's every practice," he says.

"I signed up for gymnastics, not ballet. Ballet is so boring," Trista whines.

"Trista, do you want to be a floor champion?" he asks.

"Yes," she says without hesitation.

"Then go get your tights on," he orders.

I secretly like dance, so I start walking toward our cubbies to get my tights on.

"Not so fast, Red," James says stopping me. "Do you understand what Trista showed you?"

"Yes," I confirm.

"Then let's see it," he says. "You can be late to dance."

"A whole routine or just the mil circle?" I ask.

"Let's do the whole thing since you only got two turns with me today," he says.

I start with a glide and pull over with good form, I do a nice front hip circle, I make my shoot through, and then I lift up for my mil circle. I lean forward and circle around the bar. As I am coming back up to the top again I feel my momentum slow and I almost come to a stop. James puts a hand on my back before I fall backwards and suspends me leaning back at a 45-degree angle.

"Look at your wrists," he says. I look down and see they are kind of left behind the rest of my body, not lined up with my arms. "Rotate them, please," he says. And when I do he pushes me up to be on top of the bar. "Finish," he says as he lets go of my back and steps away from me. I know he means to finish the routine. I do the basket swing, cut my leg over the bar, and finish up with my back hip circle and swing down dismount.

"Red, it's a common problem. Most people get it when they are learning the mil circle, not a year later. Don't think so much, it was working for you," he suggests.

"Yeah, okay," I agree.

"Dance," he says, and I nod. I hustle into the lobby and over to the cubbies. My teammates have already put their tights and ballet slippers on and I can hear them walking up the stairs to the second floor. I'm looking forward to dance class. It's never frustrating.

Chapter 5

Tendus in Dance

I step in the room and my team is in their usual places. Marissa and Alexis on the barre on the back wall and Savannah and Trista on the right wall, leaving the side by the window open for me. I cross the room to my lonely barre and easily pick up where they are doing tendu drills.

I slide my feet forward and back in the tendus and I take a deep breath. It feels good to let the music wash over me and let my legs move to the soothing sound of the classical music. The simple drills are easy compared to the last half hour of agony on bars. Dance is a whole lot easier than gymnastics.

"Stop, stop," Madame says, going over to her phone to pause the music. "Let's go over the arms again," she instructs. When you tendu to the front, I want your arm up here. When you tendu to the side, move your arm to the side, and when you tendu to the back, move your arm in front of you like this," she says. "Practice it slow, on your own please."

This is so basic, I'm not sure why we are going over it again. I look over at my teammates and they look genuinely frustrated and confused about the arm positions. Am I the only one that thinks dance is easy? I know that Savannah learns skills in gymnastics without even thinking about how to do it. But now I see her forehead wrinkled up in concentration harder than I have ever seen as she tries to remember the arm positions and how they go with the different feet positions.

"Yes, that's right. Tuck your bums under, shoulders down, chin up. Be proud to show your pretty faces," Madame Julia says to us as she walks around the room checking our form. "Better. Let's try again with music."

We spend a lot of time correcting our arms and working on pressing our shoulders down. This means we do a lot of tendus. I honestly don't mind doing them over and over. It's relaxing and I can feel myself growing longer and getting better with each of her corrections. But my teammates are growing weary of the repetition.

When the music ends we stop and immediately drop our tired arms. Then Madame tells us to line up in two corners of the room so we can practice leaps diagonally across the room. We are lined up in two lines waiting for the music when Katie pokes her head in. "Sorry to interrupt. Julia, may I speak to you for a quick moment?"

"Sure," she looks at us, "leaps while I am gone. On both sides," she adds. Then she walks over to Katie at the doorway and they step out of the room.

"Ugh, what a relief," Trista says. At this Alexis giggles and kicks up to handstand. Savannah starts swinging on one of the barres. It's a good thing she is miniature because I don't think the barres are meant to hold a person's weight like the uneven bars are.

"It's not so bad now that we're done with tendus," Savannah says swinging away. Marissa does a leap across the room and connects it to a cartwheel at the end.

"I'm going to do that with an aerial when I'm in Level 6," Marissa says.

"It's a cool combination," Alexis agrees, kicking up into a handstand, "but you can't do an aerial," she points out.

Marissa does the combination again, "I will when I'm a Level 6," she says mid-cartwheel.

"My combination is going to have a front aerial," Savannah says, also upside-down. She is still hanging from the barre and has put her feet between her hands and is hanging her head back to talk to us.

This is the moment Madame Julia and Katie come back in, Savannah hanging upside-down, Marissa doing her gym-acro, Alexis and Trista practicing handstand pirouettes.

Julia looks horrified at our behavior while Katie laughs. Julia looks at Katie with an expression that silently says, *what do I do? They are out of control.* Katie grins and says, "Sorry Julia, gymnasts don't like to be right side up for long periods of time." She turns on her heel and says, "Enjoy the rest of class," over her shoulder as she walks out.

We scramble back into our lines without being asked and we are trying not to giggle at Katie's explanation of our behavior. Julia eyes us for a minute like we are a different species. "You girls are like no one I have ever instructed before. But I will make dancers out of you."

I see her strength and determination and I get the feeling that we have offended her. I guess we didn't listen when she told us to do leaps, but it's more than that. She knows that my team doesn't like dance and, for some reason, this hurts her. I want to try even harder to make up for my team's constant complaints.

I do my leaps how she says, with my shoulders down, my arms in the correct position so you can see my face, my chin up and eyes down so I can see the floor in front of me. I point my toes and try to lift my legs using extension rather than quick gymnast force. I'm rewarded with, "Beautiful Paige!" This makes me feel good, it comes so easy. Now I know how Savannah and Alexis feel all the time, when things come so easy in gymnastics.

After doing right, left, and side leaps, she says, "That is enough for today . . . my little monkeys." *Did Madame Julia just crack a joke?*

"That's right!" Trista says and skips out of the room. I smile at her joke and let my teammates scrabble out the door in front of me. The room is instantly quiet with their quick departure.

"Are you a monkey at heart or a dancer Paige?" I'm surprised she asks me this. It makes me stop and think.

"I'm . . . I'm not sure," I stammer. And I'm not. I mean, I love gymnastics, but it's so much harder for me than dance. Does that mean I'm in the wrong sport?

"You don't have to know the answer today," she says with a smile. "Good job in class. Thank you for respecting dance."

I duck my head, "Thanks," I say, a little embarrassed that she is aware my team is so disrespectful to classical dance.

Chapter 6

Half Turn on Beam

"Hey pumpkin, how was practice?" my mom asks
as I climb into the car.

"Good. Well, bars was a bit of a mess, but James
was nice about it. And dance was fun. Mom, I'm really
good at dance."

"You are?" she says looking at me in the rear view mirror.

"Yeah, I mean, it's easy for me," I say.

"Well, I would imagine dance is easier in general than gymnastics," she comments.

"I thought that too, but you should see my teammates. Dance is hard for them. Which is so weird because they're good athletes."

"I guess it comes down to interest. People are usually good at what they are interested in."

"Or are they just interested in things they are good at?" I ask. "Because I'm very interested in gymnastics, but it's not easy for me like it is for Savannah and Alexis, even Trista."

"What about Marissa? Is it easy for her?" my mom asks.

"No, I think she works harder than all of us."

"Paige, you don't have to do gymnastics forever you know," my mom says.

"What? That's not what I'm saying! I love it! I'm just saying, dance is easier for me and it's a weird thing to learn about myself.

"Okay, I didn't mean to upset you, I'm just saying you can do other things if you like them better," she explains.

"Well, I don't," I confirm and I cross my arms and lean back in my seat. We drive in silence the rest of the way home.

At home my dad is playing the game *Sorry!* with my little brother, Jason. Jason is five and just started Kindergarten. He loves that game and I'm impressed he got my dad to play with him tonight.

"Hey, you two," my mom says, stepping over the board game and heading into the kitchen. She walks over to a crock pot, lifts the lid and stirs it. "I hope your game is almost over because dinner is ready," she announces.

"No way, I have three more guys to get home," Jason says.

"We can pause, buddy, and finish after dinner," my dad suggests. My brother ignores him and keeps playing while my mom sets the table.

I quickly go upstairs to throw some pajama pants on over my leotard. I walk back in the kitchen just as my mom is telling my brother he has to pause and come to the table. "Remember Jason," she cajoles, "you were excited earlier to have the family sit at the table?" she reminds him. This makes Jason jump up and run to the table.

"Daddy, sit here, sit here!" he says jumping up and down and pointing to the chair my dad always sits in. I walk over to the table to take a seat and see a whoopee cushion on my dad's chair. My dad, of course, sees the whoopee cushion too, but makes a big show of not seeing it. He lowers himself into the chair slowly and "Ffffffrrrrttt!" says the whoopee cushion. This makes us all erupt in laughter. Even though we knew it was coming. My dad makes me laugh with his pretend-embarrassed expression and my brother is doubling over in laughter. He finds this trick hysterical no matter how many times he does it.

"Daaaad! What do you say?" he yells.

"Excuse me!" my dad bellows.

"You really shouldn't fart at the table," my brother chastises, "it's rude,"

"Yeah, yeah, I think it was a set up," my dad says removing the whoopee cushion.

"How'd that get there?" Jason says with innocence. Somehow this silly act is funnier than the farting sound. My brother can be a royal pain sometimes, but he can also be so cute and funny. The laughter around the table dies down and we start to eat.

"Paige," my dad begins, "how was practice?"

"Fine," I answer.

"When is State Meet?"

"Next weekend," I answer.

"Are you ready?"

"I think so. We've been working on dance a lot lately so we look better on beam and floor. I think it's sort of cool, but my teammates hate it."

"Really? Why?" he asks.

"Why do I like it or why do they hate it?"

"Both," he answers.

"Mom," my brother interrupts, "why is the moon different each night?" he asks, pointing to the dark sky.

Sure enough, the moon tonight is different from the full moon last night.

While my mom tries to answer that question I turn to my dad, "I like it because it's relaxing and challenging at the same time. I think my teammates think it's boring."

"Why do they think it's boring?" he asks.

"Because in dance you're right side up, gymnasts like to be upside down," I grin. This makes my dad laugh and I love hearing the sound.

My brother turns and sees my dad laughing at something I said and frowns a little. He's used to being the one to make my parents laugh and I can tell he's working out what to do about my brief moment of comedic attention. "Hey, Paige, what happens if you fart during your beam routine?"

"Jason!" my mom says in surprise. Although, honestly, I'm not sure why she's surprised, the child is obsessed with farting and pooping jokes.

"Hope it's not loud so no one hears," my dad answers. I groan, now I have something new to worry about. What if I really do fart during a beam routine?

The entire arena would hear me! Up on the skinny beam all by myself it would be clear to everyone who actually ripped it. I couldn't play it off as someone else's fart.

"Oh pumpkin," my mom says seeing my face, "you won't fart during your routine, that's ridiculous."

"No it's not! It could happen, she farts all the time."

"I do not! You little twerp!" I yell, he is *so annoying!*

"Hey, hey, let's not call names," my Mom orders as I glare at my lame brother.

"So, honey," my mom says turning to my Dad, "how's work going?"

"They're doing more lay-offs, it's terrible, Phil was let go today," he says solemnly.

"Really, Phil? Wow, he's good isn't he?" my mom asks.

"One of the best," my dad mumbles into his plate. My mom's attempt to change the subject away from my brother and I fighting has lead her into an even worse topic.

"I'm sorry to hear that," she says and we eat silently for a while.

"Dad," I say, "what happens if you lose your job?" I ask.

"Oh, don't worry about me Paige, your old man will be fine," he says. Sometimes I hate it when grown-ups say that. He doesn't look fine. He looks worried and my mom looks worried. And now my worries about State Meet and farting seem so silly and I feel bad I was fighting with my brother. I decide to be good and not fight with the twerp the rest of the night. A lofty goal, but I plan to try.

Chapter 7

Tuck Jumps on Floor

"Hello Paige, what are you working tonight?" Coach Melony asks as I walk into Perfect Balance's Open Gym.

"Just getting ready for State, so routines, I guess," I answer. I'm not really sure what I want to focus on tonight, but coming in for an extra day seemed like the right thing to do before our final meet of the season.

I walk past the front desk and over to the cubbies. There I find Alexis and her brother, Drew, putting their things away too.

"Hey Paige," Alexis greets me, "what brings you in?"

"State, I guess, what about you?"

"Drew begged me to come," she answers

"I did not," he says, "I asked you to come because it would be more likely that Mom would bring us if there were two of us asking to go," he explains.

"That's true, so you owe me because I didn't really need to come tonight, I could have watched TV for once," she replies.

"Fine, I owe you, but for the record, this is more fun than TV," he smiles and walks through the doors into the training gym.

"He's right," I say, "it's more fun than TV."

"Yeah, but don't let him know that I know that. I may get a few chores out of him," she smirks.

"Hey guys," Savannah says walking up with Trista.

"Hey," we say, and for the first time, it's awkward greeting my teammates. Trista and Savannah are quiet as they put their stuff away. This is unusual for these two. They are always chattering about something.

We watch as they silently get situated and without a word go into the training area to warm up.

"That was weird," says Alexis.

"What was weird?" Carmen asks walking up and stuffing her bag in a cubby. Carmen is a Level 2 that works out with us sometimes at Open Gym and Parents' Night Out. She prefers our group because she's closer to our ages and is friends with Trista.

"Trista and Savannah are being weird," I explain.

"What do you think is going on?" Alexis asks.

"I have no idea, maybe nothing. Let's go warm up with them and see," I say as the three of us walk into the training area and over to floor.

We do tuck jumps to get our bodies going before sitting down to stretch. Once we are sitting and stretching, it's weird again that none of us are talking. Thankfully James walks up. "Hey Ladies," he says. "Last open workout before State, I don't want you coming in next Friday, the night before the meet, okay?"

"Okay," I agree since no one else says anything.

"What's going on over here? Why is it quiet?" He asks. I shrug because I genuinely don't know what's going on.

"We don't always have to get along, do we?" Trista says with sass.

"You always need to be respectful of each other," James fires back. "Got it Trista?" he adds. "Respect for your teammates, your coaches, your parents, your teachers."

"Yeah," she mumbles, "I got it." He nods accepting her words.

Then he turns to the rest of us, "Savannah, I want you to work vault. Paige bars, Alexis beam, and Trista floor dance."

"But James, isn't the point of Open Gym that we can work whatever we want?" Trista asks.

"Carmen is the only one that gets to work what she wants. The rest of you are in season and it's the week before State. That means you work what I tell you to work," he answers. When we don't say anything he nods and leaves us to go be bossy to another group of kids.

"Floor dance?" Trista says, "That's so boring," she whines.

"It's not so bad," I try.

"No, Paige, it is bad. I don't know why you're using dance to be the favorite, but it's annoying."

"I'm not using dance for anything, and I'm not the favorite," I say. So that's her problem, and Savannah knows it too.

"You've ruined everything!" She huffs. I'm shocked that somehow I'm the one that has ruined 'everything.'

"I signed up for gymnastics, not dance, and I'm tired of boring dance," Trista exclaims. Then she stalks over to the mirrors on floor to work on her dance.

"What was that?" I ask Savannah. "She's like her own personal storm."

"She thinks that we have to do all this dance because of you," Savannah explains.

"Because of me? That's crazy." I say, truly baffled.

"I know. I told her it was dumb. But she thinks that since James and Julia see how it can look on you, that they are pushing us to look the same. She thinks that if you were bad at dance too, no one would expect so much out of us."

"Has she seen the other teams? They do look better than us on floor," I point out.

"Yeah, but she still scores well because of her tumbling, so she thinks it's a waste," Alexis adds. "Why don't I talk to her?" she asks, looking at Savannah.

"Go ahead, I've tried, she is acting like a Dra – I mean, a bit over the top," Savannah stammers out. *What was Savannah about to say? Dra – what? Dra? Drama? Drama Queen?*

"Drama Queen?" I laugh. "You were going to say Drama Queen! That's so perfect!"

"Shh! Paige! If that name catches on in the gym she is going to be so mad at me," Savannah confesses.

"It's perfect, we were going to come around to calling her that eventually," I justify.

"You better not let her hear you say it. She will never forgive either of us," Savannah pleads.

"Yeah, okay . . . but it's still funny," I insist and Savannah agrees with a shrug and a little smile.

Chapter 8

Split Leap on Beam

"Five stuck routines," James says. We are at our
Monday workout and we just finished our warm up
complex on beam. There are four high beams and
five of us. One person has to sit out, and as soon as
someone finishes a routine the person waiting jumps
up on the newly empty beam. Today I'm first to sit out.
I'm standing next to James watching my team. My

teammates look good; more bold in their movements than at the beginning of the season.

I watch Alexis prepare for her leap down the beam and she does the highest leap I have ever seen her do. Except when she goes to put her foot on the beam for the landing, her foot is off to the side by about two inches, catching only her big toe onto the beam. Her big toe can't hold her and her foot slides down the side of the beam, scrapping her inner leg all the way down until *slam!* She hits the beam between her legs as her body swings to the side and as she is falling to the side her other leg smacks the beam before she slams onto her back under the beam. The sound ricochets throughout the gym and for a moment everyone in the gym has stopped to look over at beam.

Our team is in stunned silence as Alexis curls to her side, crying. James runs to her and tells her to breathe. "Red, ice! The rest of you, back to work on the far beams."

I run through the doors that connect the training area directly to the office.

"What do you need, hon?" Samantha, one of the receptionists, asks.

"Ice," I say a little frantically.

"In the freezer," she says gesturing to the full size freezer across the room by Katie's desk. "And grab a towel," she says.

I walk across the room, swing open the freezer and grab a bag of ice. I see a stack of clean towels on the desk next to the freezer and I grab one.

"Everything okay out there?" Samantha asks.

"Alexis straddled beam," I say.

"Is she okay?" she asks, making sure this is not a serious injury.

"I think so," I answer quickly and walk back out into the training area.

I get over to the beams and give the ice and towel to James. Alexis is sitting up and she is crying and rocking back and forth. James takes the ice bag from me and wraps it in the towel I give him. "Can you move over here?" he asks, "so you're not under the beams?" She sniffles and nods. He helps her up, walks with her over to a panel mat by the medium beam.

She sits down and he hands her the ice. She takes it and applies it to her upper inner thigh with a wince. Her entire leg is red and I can see red welts and bruises already forming.

"Well, Lexi, you are officially a beam worker," James says. "Your first beam straddle. It was a good one. That was go big or go home." This makes Alexis try for a smile, but I can see she is in too much pain to think it's cool yet.

"That was a really pretty leap," I try.

James smiles at me, "It was a really pretty leap, nice and high, that's why you were off on the landing, you weren't used to it."

"Then I'm never doing one that big again," she croaks out around her tears.

"Yeah, you will. Today, in fact. Before we rotate to dance," he informs her. "In about 15 minutes when your leg is done icing we'll try again."

"What? No. James, I can't. Not today, please," she begs.

"Red," James says to me, "thanks for the ice, now back to your beam assignment," he orders. I hesitate, feeling bad for Alexis, but I do as I'm told and head over to the high beams to do my assignment.

I climb up onto the beam next to Trista.

"How's she doing?" Trista says to me from the next beam over. She has stopped doing her routine and is looking at me with real concern. It's hard for me to stay frustrated with Trista when she looks so worried for Alexis.

"Pretty banged up," I say. "Did you see it?"

"Out of the corner of my eye, but I was in the middle of a routine, so not really. You did though, huh? Because you were waiting for a beam?" she asks.

"Yeah, I saw it. It was bad. She scraped her entire leg before hitting the beam."

"Ladies!" we hear James yell. And that's all it takes, we know to resume our routines without any more talking.

Chapter 9

Cartwheel on Low Beam

Savannah finishes her five stuck routines and jumps down announcing to James that she's done.

"You can work cartwheels on low beam," James says to Savannah. Then he turns to Alexis, who is still sitting by the medium beam icing her leg, and says, "Alexis, a beam is open."

We all look at Alexis with sympathy. It seems so mean to make Alexis walk on her banged up legs, much less walk on a beam.

She slowly gets up and limps over to a beam and climbs up. James tells her to do forward and backward walks. She does and then stops and looks at him questioningly.

"Your leap," he says. Alexis takes a deep breath and takes a few steps down the beam and does the tiniest leap I have ever seen. In fact, it looked more like a large step.

"I said your leap," says James, relentlessly.

"I did," she squeaks, knowing it was pathetic.

"No, you didn't."

"I can't do it," she says with tears starting to form in her eyes. "Please don't make me. It really hurts."

James sighs, "I know it hurts, Lex," he says quietly. "But you can't let beam get to you. You have to learn to be mentally tough on beam. One leap, one real leap. That's all I need you to do."

"I can't," she says, and her tears begin rolling down her face.

"When you come in on Wednesday," he continues, as if she isn't crying, "you won't have any worries, you'll know you can do it."

This is a nice pep talk, but Alexis doesn't look convinced and now her face is getting red and blotchy, she is sniffing her nose, and trying to take a deep breath.

James looks at the rest of us. Of course, we have stopped to watch what will happen. "It's time for dance ladies. Go put on your tights and head upstairs. Lex will be up in a minute." We do as we are told and jump off the beams and start walking to the cubbies so we can change into our tights.

Just then Drew walks by from the drinking fountain. "What's going on over here? What are you doing to my sister?" he asks.

"Drew, I'm not hurting her. Beam did it all on its own," James replies dryly.

Drew doesn't look convinced, so I help him understand. "She straddled beam on a leap. Look at the bruises on her legs."

"Seriously? Oh man," he says glimpsing the bright red welts on her legs. "I'm glad beam isn't a boys' event. You okay?" he asks. Alexis silently nods from up on her beam, but the tears are still coming.

"Please don't cry sis, it's over, right?" She brushes at her tears with the back of her hand and nods again. I can tell she is trying really hard not to let new tears fall, but they are coming anyway. Drew studies her for a minute. "Do you want me to call Mom?" he asks quietly. She shakes her head, no.

"I'll talk to her when she comes to get you guys," James says. "Back to work Drew." Drew gives Alexis one last look and heads back over to the boys' events. I am touched at how a brother would help his sister like that. I wonder if Jason will be that nice to me when he is older.

"Red, go to dance," James says, shaking me out of my thoughts. I turn and go out into the lobby.

At the cubbies the girls are talking about Alexis as they put on their tights. "Do you think she'll do her leap today?" Trista asks.

"I hope so," Marissa replies.

"Why?" asks Savannah.

"Because we need her on Saturday," Marissa says.

We need her on Saturday. Wow, Marissa is right. I forgot that all of our scores will be added up to get a team score. Wouldn't that be so great if we could be the Level 3 Champions of Utah? I wonder if we have a real chance. I have been so caught up thinking about my shot as an individual that I forgot that we can win as a team. I smile to myself, that seems a whole lot more likely, and easier!

I walk up to dance with visions of the five of us holding a huge trophy and James with a goofy dad grin on his face.

"So what happened, Lex?" Trista asks.

We finished our dance rotation and practice is over for tonight. This is the first chance we have to talk to each other since dance started. Naturally, the first thing we want to know is how beam went for Alexis after we went upstairs.

"I did it," she mumbles as she stuffs her arms in the sleeves of her purple sweatshirt.

"You did?" Trista says. "Wow, I probably wouldn't have," she admits.

Alexis frowns and says, "Well, I did lots of tiny leaps and one medium leap. James was so fed up with me he accepted the medium leap and let me go up to dance," she explains.

"Do you feel okay about beam now?" Trista asks as she pulls on her yoga pants over her leotard.

"Not really," Alexis says.

Drew sticks his head into the lobby from outside and yells to us, "Mom's here Lex, let's go." We watch her limp over to her brother and disappear through the doors.

"She looks miserable," Savannah observes and we silently nod in agreement.

Chapter 10

Leg Swings on Floor

"Today you will not be doing traditional ballet for dance class," James announces. "Madame Julia is going to work with you on your floor routines down here."

"Yay!" Trista blurts out. "Can we tumble extra if we finish early?" she asks.

"Trista, you're missing what I'm saying. You are going to work floor *dance*, not floor tumbling. State is on Saturday and you guys are ready. Time for a little polish."

"Oh," She says deflated. This makes me giggle a little. "What, Paige?" she says to me with a scowl.

"You're funny, dance isn't that bad," I say.

"For you –, " she starts but James cuts her off.

"We all have our favorite event," he says as Julia walks up. "Marissa, show Julia a floor routine so she knows what leaps and jumps to work on, Paige que the music." I walk over to the gym ipod and stereo system. I select the Level 3 music and as it begins so does Marissa.

After Marissa is done Julia lines us up in front of the mirrors along the floor and we practice our split jumps, leaps, poses, arm positions, everything in our routine. She makes us press our shoulders down and extend our necks, put our chin up, and make our fingers graceful. After 30 minutes I am exhausted from trying to remember everything, and I like dance. I look over to my teammates to see how they are doing. They are trying so hard; Marissa even has her tongue out in concentration. They look good. They look really good. Julia knows what she's doing.

"Okay girls, let's try it in your routine. You don't have to do the gymnastics parts unless you want to." Our routine is a simple up and back in a straight line on the floor. We each take a section of the floor and all five us can do our routine at once. "I want to see one good one from each of you. Then you're done. But we'll all keep going until everyone looks good," she explains.

"Wait, so if I do a good routine, but Savannah doesn't, I have to do it again?" Trista clarifies.

"Yes. So do your teammates a favor and get it right as soon as possible," she says, and heads over to start the music.

"Let's do this once, okay guys?" Marissa pleads. And then the music begins.

On the first three routines we all did the gymnastics parts; back roll to push-up position, bridge kick over, and round off back handspring. By the fourth routine we started petering out. Julia would not tell us who still had to do a decent routine, just that one of us still had to 'find her performance quality.' By six routines she let us be done. I'm not sure all of us found our performance quality or if she just gave up.

"We're done?" Savannah asks.

"Savannah! Don't question the lady, she said done, let's be done," Trista says.

"Yes, you girls are done with dance throughs. Work on your turns while I go get James."

We half-heartedly work our turns in front of the mirror, but mostly we are just standing around.

"This is it guys," Marissa says, "we just finished our last workout before state."

"Wow," Alexis says, "I can't believe it's this Saturday." We are quiet for a second as that thought sinks in.

"Ladies," James says walking up to us, "no conditioning tonight, I'm going to talk to you while you stretch." No conditioning? We always have conditioning. "Grab a panel mat for over-splits while we talk." We do as he says and grab a panel mat and drag it to the edge of the floor where he is standing. He sits on the mat and we each put a foot up on the mat and slide into over-splits. We look at him expectantly.

"As you all know, Saturday is State Meet. I do not want to see anyone here for Open Gym or PNO on Friday. I want you in bed early and rested. Got it?" We nod. "I want you to eat healthy and show up healthy, okay?" We nod again. "Any questions?"

"Can I scratch beam?" Alexis asks.

"What? No." James answers.

"But Trista gets to scratch bars, I want to scratch beam. Please James, I'm not ready on beam," Alexis pleads.

"Alexis you are ready on beam. You just had a hard crash this week," he answers.

"But why does Trista get to scratch?" Alexis presses.

"Because I am terrible at bars!" Trista interjects. "You're not bad at beam, Alexis, it's different." Watching this I feel bad for Trista, I don't think Alexis meant to insult her. She just really wants out of beam.

"Alexis we are trying for a team placement on Saturday and we need you on beam, okay?" James asks.

"Okay," she mumbles.

"Anything else?" he asks.

"What order are we?" Marissa asks, referring to what order we will be competing the four events.

"It will be drawn that morning, so I don't know yet," James answers. "But that reminds me, it will not be Capital Cup format like we have been doing all season. It will be a traditional format."

"What's Capital Cup?" Marissa asks.

"It's what we have been doing all season. Where we march in, then warm up, compete, warm up, compete. On Saturday we will warm up every event, march in, then compete every event with a quick one touch warm up," James explains.

"That sounds hard," Trista says, and I agree with her. I like warming up an event and then competing it.

"It can be, but it's better for spectators. It's common in State Meets and higher level meets,"

James looks around at us. "Any other questions about Saturday?"

"How many count toward the team score?" Savannah asks.

"They will take our best three scores on each event and add them up for the team score," James answers.

"What about the teams that have, like, fifteen kids? That doesn't seem fair." Marissa points out. Leave it to Marissa to understand the odds of this system right away.

"The bigger teams will designate their team Saturday morning. They will have to pick four or five girls whose scores are allowed to be used for the team score. The meet directors try to make it as fair as possible. But you are right, bigger teams have a small advantage," James agrees.

We are silent so he says, "Okay, well, I think you ladies are ready. I'll see you Saturday morning, you are free to go."

"We didn't even change sides," Savannah says as we get out of our splits.

"Savannah!" Trista chides. "Why would you remind him?"

James laughs, "You guys can still go. Finish your stretches at home," he says. We all know none of us will do that, including James.

Chapter 11

The Night Before State Meet

 "I'll get it!" I yell as I slide around the corner of our kitchen into the entry way. I'm expecting my teammates over any moment. Since we can't go to Parents' Night Out tonight my mom let me invite my team over for movie night. Movie Night is something my mom has been doing every Friday night since Jason and I were little. We order pizza and watch a movie. Actually, I get to watch two movies since I'm older than Jason. We watch a movie with him, then he goes to bed, and I get to pick a movie that's not a cartoon.

Tonight there will be no second movie because we need go to bed early. The moms agreed to let us get together as long as everyone goes home by nine.

I swing open the door with a big smile and there stands the pizza delivery guy. "Oh," I say, "let me get the money." I grab the money off the entry way table that my mom laid out and hand it to him.

I barely get a thanks from him as he hands me the pizza box and runs off the porch. I don't blame him. There are flurries of snow floating and swirling around and I see steam coming off the pizza box as I hold it in the cool air of the entry way.

With his departure I slam the door shut and yell to my family, "Pizza's here!" I carry the box to the kitchen and set it down. As soon as I set it down the doorbell rings again. This time it has to be my friends. I go careening back around the corner in my stocking feet on the hardwood floor.

This time when I open the door Marissa and Alexis are on the porch. "Hey guys!" I say backing up so they can come in.

"Paige! Your hair looks so pretty down like that!" Alexis exclaims.

"Cool jeans," Marissa adds. "I'm not used to seeing you in clothes," Marissa says and we all laugh. We know what she means. We only ever see each other in leotards and shorts with our hair pulled up. It's fun to see these girls outside the gym.

"Wanna see my room?" I ask and they nod and we all run up.

"Ooh, I love the purple and teal," Alexis squeals. "Mine is pink everything," she adds

"My mom says red heads should stay away from pink," I say.

"My mom was so happy to have a girl that every spot on my room is pink. It's even worse than Savannah's room," Alexis observes.

"I love the medals over here," Marissa says walking over to my book shelf. I have my three medals looped around soccer and softball trophies and hanging down. They are about at Marissa's eye level.

"You did soccer?" she says looking at the trophies.

"And softball?"

"Yeah, before gymnastics. But I was always doing cartwheels on the field during games when it got boring so my parents gave up on me and put me in gymnastics," I explain.

"I've only done chess club, music, and theatre. No other sports," Marissa comments. She reaches out to touch my medals. She flips them over to read the back. Sometimes at meets they print the person's name, event, score, and placement on a sticky label and stick it to the back of the medal or ribbon.

"30.95, eighth place All-Around," she reads. Then she flips over the next one, "31.35, sixth place, All-Around," and the last one, "31.75, tenth place, All-Around." She looks at me, "I didn't realize all of your awards are from the All-Around. Mine are too," she comments.

"Yeah," I say, not sure what to say. Marissa is one of my biggest threats to winning the All-Around and it is an odd feeling to want to beat a teammate, a friend.

"But you're so good at floor," Alexis says, "have you been messing up floor?" Sometimes Alexis expresses herself like her brothers and I find that I like the honesty and directness.

"Not really, I just have a hard time with the round off back handspring and the bridge kick over."

"Think you'll place in the All-Around tomorrow?" Marissa asks.

"I don't know about that, State is a harder meet," I say. But secretly, I really, really, want to get in the top ten All-Around tomorrow.

"I think you've gotten better on floor than you think," Alexis says as she picks up a bobby pin with a firefly on the end and puts it in her hair. "How does it look?"

I look at her sleek blond bob and I love how the firefly sparkles just above her eyebrow and pulls her hair up and out of her eyes. I'm so jealous. Her hair falls perfectly straight and frames her face. "Really cute," I answer honestly. "You can borrow it if you want," I offer.

"Really?" she says, "I wish I had sisters to share stuff with." She studies herself in the mirror turning her head to let the firefly catch and shine in the light.

"You don't wish you had sisters," Marissa adds, "My sister just takes everything and calls it borrowing," she complains.

The doorbell rings interrupting our conversation. We all run down the stairs to meet Savannah and Trista.

We open the door and Savannah looks adorable with a sparkling pink sweatshirt with the words Gymnast on it. Under her arm she is holding a bunch of magazines.

"You seriously look like Merida from Brave with your hair down," Trista says. I smile in response.

The girls come in and my mom herds us into the kitchen to make us eat the pizza 'that has been sitting there getting cold.'

My mom asks us about the meet tomorrow and how we feel about it.

"Paige is going to win the All-Around," Alexis says playfully, "Trista is going to win floor, Marissa is going to win beam, and Savannah what are you going to win?"

Savannah's eyes get wide and she shrugs, "I don't know, what am I good at? Not beam."

Trista rolls her eyes, "Everything, Savannah, all the events are pretty easy for you."

"But I keep falling on beam," she says.

"Well, not tomorrow, I know you are going to stick beam tomorrow," Trista says.

"Based on process of elimination, vault and bars are left. You would probably win bars over vault, Savannah. That leaves Alexis winning vault," Marissa logically points out.

"That would be so cool," Alexis says.

We are quiet for a minute as we fantasize about all of us winning an event.

"But Twisters will be there, and St. George Gymnastics, and Aerials, and Salt Lake Gymnastics..." Marissa says, ruining our fantasy.

"Yeah, they're good," Alexis agrees.

"So are we!" Trista cheers.

"Let's just do our best and see what happens," I say. I can tell the turn in conversation to the other teams has upset Savannah. She seems the most affected by competition.

After we finish eating pizza my brother announces we are watching Zootopia. We decide to hang out in my room instead since we've all seen that movie.

On the way up to my room I stop at the game closet to see if we want to play something. "Ooh, I love Sorry!" Savannah says, as we stare at the closet.

"Five can't play Sorry," Alexis says.

"Clue?" Trista asks.

"Four again," Alexis says.

"You have chess way up there; anyone want to play chess with me?" Marissa asks.

"Can you teach me?" Alexis asks.

"Sure," Marissa says. Hearing this I reach up and get the chess game down for them since I know I'm the only one tall enough to get it. I hand it to Marissa and turn back to looking at the games.

"What do you two want to do?" I ask Savannah and Trista.

"*Clue!* Please Savannah, we play *Sorry* all the time at your house," Trista pleads.

"Okay," Savannah says and I get down *Clue* and we all head up to my room.

A half hour later Marissa and Alexis are still on the floor of my room playing their first game of chess. Trista and Savannah are playing a second game of Clue. I played the first game with them, but I didn't want to play a second time like they did. I'm lying on my stomach, sideways on my bed, flipping through the magazines Savannah brought over. She brought International Gymnast Magazine and some Gymkin Catalogs. I see the sweatshirt Savannah is wearing in the catalogue and now I know where she gets her cute gymnastics themed clothing. I look up and watch Savannah and Trista engrossed in their game. Those two are really close. They are lucky to be neighbors.

Then I look over at Marissa and Alexis and they are into their game too. "No, the only one that can go over people is the knight," Marissa says.

"The horse?" Alexis asks.

"Yeah, but the horse is called a knight," Marissa explains.

"But why is he the only one that gets to skip over everyone? I think the queen should be able to do that too. I mean, she *is* the *queen*." Alexis reasons.

This makes Marissa laugh, "Maybe you're right, but that's not how the game goes. Try something else."

As I watch my team on the floor playing games I realize I'm the odd girl out and this makes me a little sad. I guess I've been feeling this way for a while. I'm the only one that likes dance and I always have to partner with a girl from the non-competitive Level 3 group during conditioning. I never carpool to practice like they do. At practice they are always talking about their friends and siblings and I'm never really up on what is going on. I flip through a few more pages of the Gymkin Catalogue. I see famous gymnasts in beautiful leotards with perfect muscles staring back at me. Did these gymnasts ever care if they were an accepted part of their team?

Sometimes I feel like I am standing to the side watching my team, like I am now, rather than sitting in the middle being with my team.

Where do I fit in?

Chapter 12

Bridge Kick Over on Floor

"Paige, you are the leader of this team and I need you to help me out with this," James pleads.

We were stretching on the floor at State Meet along with the other teams when James came up to me with his impossible request.

"Paige, can you come with me for a second?" James asked me.

I am surprised by James' request, but I stand up and come with him, he walks off the floor and over to the back of the arena, away from the parents.

He stops by the bars and says, "Okay, here's the deal. I thought this meet was going to be four girls compete and three scores count. And I was going to have to designate four of you to represent PBGA."

"That's terrible! How were you going to pick?" I ask, surprised coaches have to do things like that.

"It is hard," James admits, "but with Trista not competing on bars yet, it was an easy decision to leave her off the team roster and just let her compete for herself on three events. Now all of you need to compete on everything. Five girls up, four scores count."

"But there are only five of us," I say in shock. "That doesn't seem fair, the bigger teams have an advantage."

"Well, they have to designate which five competitors' scores count. They have a small advantage, but not much. Look, we don't have time to talk about the fairness or un-fairness of gymnastics.

"I have to get to the head table and change Trista's bars status from scratch to compete and get back to the team before timed warms ups begin. Trista needs to know why she has to do bars. Let her know her routine doesn't have to be perfect. Maybe tell her away from the others first," he suggests. "Since she's not here yet I need you to tell her while I'm making the changes with the meet director."

"He moves to leave and sees I have not really responded. "What?" he asks.

"Well, I'm not that close to Trista, maybe Savannah should tell her," I suggest.

"I need you to do it," he responded.

I stood there looking at James, not agreeing, but not disagreeing either. I didn't make a move toward my team. I felt glued to the spot I was standing on. I didn't want to deliver this news to Trista or the team. That is when he said it, *"Paige, you are the leader of this team and I need you to help me out with this."*

He stares at me for a moment and adds, "You don't have to be the best friend to be the leader.

You just have to be respected. Go talk to Trista, then the team."

How can I say no to that? I slowly feel myself nodding. James gives me a half grin, nods, and walks off to the judges table.

He left me standing there stunned. I'm the leader? How did that happen? Because I'm the oldest? What did James say? I'm respected?

I slowly make my way back to where my team is stretching. I see Trista has arrived and she is doing the last of her tuck jumps before sliding into splits with the rest of the team.

"What was that all about?" Marissa asks.

"Umm," I stumble. Was I supposed to talk to the team first, or Trista first? I can't remember. What would I want if I was Trista?

"Trista, can I talk to you for a second?" I ask. I'm expecting some of Trista's sass but she must have seen the seriousness on my face because she just said sure and stood up. We walk off of the floor and over to the beams where it is quiet.

She looks at me expectantly.

"So here's the deal. James thought that the meet today was going to be four girls up three scores count. Now it is five girls up, four scores count," I say, hoping she will just figure out what I am saying.

"Okay. Thanks for the update. Should we tell the others?" she says. I can tell she hasn't figured out what I'm telling her.

"Trista. We need you to compete bars," I blurt out.

"Bars?" she whispers.

"Yeah. Trista, you can do it. It's not so bad," I try.

"Dance is 'not so bad.' Bars are a nightmare. Paige, I never make my shoot through or my mil circle."

We stand there in silence for a second. I don't know what to say to her.

"I will fall. Twice. I can't do it," she decides.

"We need you to," I finally say, "even if you fall."

Trista starts biting the hang nail on her pinky finger and looks up at the stands and shakes her head. "Look at all these people," she says, "I can't do bars in front of all these people."

"Trista, all those people are just parents. It's not like your crush is here or something. That would be embarrassing." I see her face go pale and her eyes are huge. I'm not sure why, so I continue, "You just have to do bars in front of parents," I say, trying to convince her this is no big deal.

Trista just looks at me with that ghostly face and now I feel bad I'm trying to make her do something she doesn't want to do.

"Drew," she whispers.

"What?" I ask.

"My crush is Drew. And I'm guessing he will be here. To see me fall on bars." She looks at me and I am shocked her crush is Alexis' brother and that she shared this huge secret with me. Now I realize I just totally made things worse by mentioning that a crush would be the only embarrassing scenario.

"Gymnasts, timed warm ups begin in 5 minutes," the meet director announces over the loud speaker. We don't have much time.

"Trista, forget Drew, although now that I think about it, he is pretty cute."

"Paige!" she shrieks.

"Sorry," I giggle. "Okay, you have to do this, we have to tell the team, and we have to get our hineys to the first event," I say. I grab her hand and walk us back over to our team.

"What the heck is going on?" Marissa asks.

I look at Trista, "You tell them," I say.

She blows out a breath and says with her head down, "I have to compete bars."

"Yay!" Savannah says, clapping her hands together, "Now you can get an All-Around score!"

"Why?" Alexis says, "I would totally scratch if I were you." We know Alexis is thinking about her dreaded beam routine.

"Five girls make a team at State Meet," I explain. "Five girls up, four scores count."

"But we only have five girls!" Marissa points out the obvious. "That's not fair," she says looking around at the other groups stretching on the floor. They are mostly groups of 10 to 15 girls, and suddenly I know we are all feeling overwhelmed.

"Hey, you guys, don't worry about them. We've got this," I say.

"Well said Red," James says walking up with papers in his hand. "I have your order. Beam, floor, vault, bars."

Savannah and Alexis groan and Marissa is delighted.

"Why are you happy about beam first?" Alexis asks.

"Because we get it over with," Marissa answers smartly.

"Which means," James continues, "we warm up floor, vault, bars, and end on beam so we are ready over there. Put your sweats away and meet me back over here," he instructs.

We go to our bags to put our things away. Very few parents are here since warm-ups are supposed to take an hour. Savannah's mom, however, has stayed to watch warm-ups and she saw something was going on.

"What does that mean?" I hear Mrs. Collins ask Savannah.

"It means Trista has to do bars and she wasn't planning on it," Savannah explains.

"What does it mean for you?" Mrs. Collins asks.

"Nothing, I guess, it's the same for me," Savannah answers.

"Oh good. Well, don't let Trista's stress bother you. You go get 'em honey! My phone is charged and ready!" I see Savannah give a weak smile, stuff her jacket the rest of the way in her bag and turn back to the floor.

"Spread out on the floor and each take a strip to practice your routine once through," James instructs. "Then I want you to do two of each skill and be done. We have 15 minutes." We are used to timed warm ups at meets so we get going and don't stop to talk to each other.

Floor warm ups are fine. We are fine. We are going to be great.

Chapter 13

Huddle Before March In

We are going to be a disaster. We are in the hallway waiting to march in and my team is close to hysterical. They are all talking at once.

"My mom is going to kill me if I compete the way I warmed up." (Savannah)

"Hey look, Carmen is here - holy cow Alexis, your whole family came?" (Trista)

"I can't do beam, I can't. Look at my legs, they're covered in purple and green bruises. Why would you guys make me do beam?" (Alexis)

"I think Salt Lake Gymnastics has, like, 20 kids. Five of them are bound to stick every event." (Marissa)

"PBGA! Huddle up!" They are surprised by my outburst and stop talking. I grab Trista and Savannah and put my arms around them. Alexis and Marissa join us and our circle is complete.

Now that I have their attention, I'm not sure what to say.

"Look, we are all nervous," I start. "Let's just do what we do in practice and see what happens. Let's have fun. Let's not worry about anyone else; not other teams, not people in the stands, just us. Okay?"

"What are you nervous about?" Trista asks me, "You seem so calm."

"I'm afraid you're never going to speak to me again when I beat you on floor," I fire back at her. I didn't mean to say something so sassy, but thank goodness Trista is laughing.

"May the best competitor win, Paige," Trista says with a grin, and somehow I know we are over all of our weirdness of the last few weeks in the gym.

Seeing that the other teams are lined up and ready for march in, Marissa says, "Okay guys, group squeeze and then we've got to get in line." We are silly and loud while we try to hug all at once until finally a meet coordinator breaks us up.

"PBGA, who is your line leader?" she asks us.

"Me," Savannah says and the meet coordinator starts talking to her about where to walk during the march in.

When she is done talking to Savannah, we line up in order without much commotion because we know what order to stand in by now. We have been lining up and marching in all season. Our line starts with Savannah, then Marissa, Trista, Alexis, and me.

The Olympic themed music begins and we watch the teams before us march out onto the floor. Then Savannah leads us in and we march over to the floor where we split off into our line facing the bleachers. For the first time there is a crowd. There are a lot of competitors, so it makes sense that there are a lot of parents. There are teams from Salt Lake City, Park City, St. George, Logan, and many other cities from Utah that I don't recognize. Our little team from Snowcap Canyon is the smallest team. This makes me nervous, we are all going to have to do really well if we want to bring home a team trophy for James and PBGA.

The teams, coaches, and judges are introduced, then a little girl in pig tails steps up to sing the national anthem. She surprises us all with her big voice and for a moment I am so captivated I forgot to worry about my team. As soon as the girl finishes singing the crowd erupts in applause; they loved her.

Then the meet director tells us to march to our first event. Savannah is used to leading us around meets and she walks confidently over to beam and we follow her. She walks us over to James. He is standing at one end of the beam and another coach is at the other end. I see that the other coach is dressed in khaki pants and a red colored shirt with an Aerials Gymnastics logo on the front pocket.

"We are rotating with Aerials?" Marissa observes.

"Yep, and with St. George Gymnastics. There are ten teams here. That means two to three in each event. Except Salt Lake, they have so many kids they rotate on their own."

"Wow, so how many kids on each event?" Alexis

"About 20, we have 21 in our rotation, 8 from Aerials, 8 from St. George and 5 of us," James answers.

While James is answering Alexis' question I see the Aerials team jump up on the beam one at a time. They each do a half turn and a dismount.

"James, are we going to do that?" I ask.

He looks over to where I am pointing up to the beams.

"Get a one touch? Yes, after Aerials compete, you are going to have a 2-minute block as a team to get on the beam and warm up your body real fast.

For now, present yourself to the head judge and come back and sit over here."

"Which one is the head judge?" I ask looking at the four judges surrounding the beam. At the other meets this season there have been one or two judges at each event, not four.

"Why are there four?" Marissa asks.

"This is State Meet; big competitions use four judges. The head judge is the one with the green flag and the ipad in front of her. That's how she sends scores to the head table over there," he says, pointing to a long table in front of the bleachers. There are about six people in navy suits behind computers.

"Okay, you guys, I'll answer more questions when you come back, but right now you need to go say hello to your beam judge," he says pushing us.

The beam judge is young and pretty. She has huge brown eyes and tons of dark hair falling down her shoulders. As I look at her perfect smile, I recognize her from somewhere.

"Good Morning ladies," she says.

"You get beam out of the way first thing, lucky draw," she says smiling. This makes my team giggle, since that is exactly what we were thinking. "Good luck today ladies," she says and we say thank you, salute her, and hustle back to James.

Chapter 14

Dismount on Beam

The first girl from Aerials is already standing by the side of the beam, ready to go.

"Do we know her? The beam judge?" I ask James.

"She's Megan Cruz from the University of Utah Gymnastics Team," Savannah supplies, "she was a senior last year."

"How do you know that, shrimp?" I ask, looking down at Savannah as we get seated.

"My mom takes me to all the University of Utah meets. And last year she was the PAC-12 Beam Champion. We went to that too," Savannah explains.

"Wow, that's intimidating," I say as I learn the celebrity status of our beam judge.

"Don't be intimidated by her," James says. "She knows better than anyone what you're going through. She was a Level 3 once too," he says. I think about this for a moment. *She was a Level 3 once too.* Does that mean I could be a college gymnast someday too?

"Look how perfect she is," Savannah breathes as we watch the first girl compete on the Aerials Team.

"Alright, listen up, I'm going to tell you your order," James says.

"I want to go first!" Trista says quickly. Trista always wants to go first and the rest of us don't want to.

"It's State Meet, I don't get to pick the order. Meet officials create the order randomly for us," James explains.

"Oh," Trista says a little deflated, "but I really want to get this meet started," she says.

"Well here we go," he says looking down at a printed out sheet he got from the head table, "Trista, ironically, you are up first, then Alexis, Paige, Savannah, and Marissa. Sit in that order and warm up in that order," James instructs. We shuffle around so we are sitting on the mats in the order he just called out.

We finally get settled and are watching the Aerials Team. Their routines are clean and they do some of the dance moves slightly different than us, but basically, it's the same. Then their last competitor steps up, she is teeny tiny. Her head doesn't even clear the top of the beam, which means she is smaller than four feet tall, and she looks about four years old.

"Is she allowed to be here this young?" I whisper to James.

"You just have to be six by the last qualifying meet, she could have turned six last week for all we know," Savannah supplies.

"How do you know?" I ask her.

Savannah shrugs, "I just know because my mom wanted me to compete last year when I was six," she explains. I look at the girl standing by the beam. She has round little baby legs instead of the lean muscles that most of us have. Her belly sticks out a little like my brother's. It looks cute on her.

I watch as she salutes the judge and has to stand on a panel mat to reach the beam and swing herself up into her mount. We watch stunned for a minute along with the rest of the arena. So she is barely six? Holy cow! This girl who just did a perfect handstand on beam is the same age as my brother. There is no way my brother could even walk on the beam. But she is up there doing it with what looks like no concern in the world.

"She *is* really cute," Savannah comments as we watch this mini-gymnast. I peer at Savannah's perfect profile as she watches this baby-child do a leap.

"You're really cute too," I say, and I tug on Savannah's pony tail. She grins up at me all blue eyes and round cheeks herself. In that moment, I feel like a giant. I mean, here I am competing with 6 and

7-year-olds and I'm a 10-year-old fifth grader. I wish I would have started gymnastics sooner instead of messing around with softball and soccer when I was Savannah's age.

The baby-child does her leap and when she lands she wobbles as she steps forward. The wobble throws her off balance and then she falls off to the side. The entire arena says, "Awwh." The audience loves her and wants her to do well. She stands stunned for a minute and looks at her coach. Her coach walks over to her and quietly tells her to climb back up and finish.

This is the funny part; the girl has to walk over to the end of the beam to climb up using the base bar of the beam rather than just jumping up in the middle like the rest of us can do. And we can all see why. The beam is so big and high up for her. She finally gets up and finishes her routine and the applause is twice as loud as it was for any other competitors so far.

"So that's what 'cute points' are," I hear Savannah say to herself as the baby-child-mini-gymnast salutes the judges.

"We're up for one touch," James says. As we stand up he adds, "Do two skills and the dismount. Know what you are going to do before you jump up. Timer is on," he says, and Trista jumps up.

Chapter 15

Swing Mount on Beam

We complete our one touch without any problems, and all of us sit back down except for Trista, who is waiting to start her routine.

The pretty judge salutes Trista and Trista gives her a giant smile and starts her routine with confidence. Trista is so brave. I don't understand how she always wants to go first up on every event. And she seems to do better in meets than in practice.

"Paige," I hear James whisper to me without taking his eyes off of Trista on beam.

"Yeah?" I whisper back.

"Go talk to Alexis," he orders. I look around and Alexis is not sitting in our line. I look behind me and I see her pacing up and back behind us between the beam and floor. Talk to Alexis? What am I supposed to say? What would James say? I stand up and walk to where Alexis is wearing a hole in the ground.

"Alexis?" I say and grab her shoulder, I look into her eyes and she looks terrified.

"I can't do it. Don't make me do it," she rushes out.

"Alexis, we need you," I say while she is shaking her head at me. I see Trista finish her routine out of the corner of my eye and James gives her a quick high five and heads over to us.

"Alexis, breathe," James says bending down to her level. "Lex. Look at me. Lexi, it doesn't have to be perfect, just get up there and do your routine. Get up there and pretend you are in the gym. You can do this. Breath Lex," he says again and I can see her face is getting some color back into it. "You can do this, okay?"

"What if I fall?" she squeaks out.

"So you fall. So what? You get up and finish. And you still get a score and we need a score, okay? Any score. I need you to be brave. I need you to go do your routine." She starts to nod and I can see he catches the eye of the judge and she nods to him. He takes Alexis by the shoulder and steers her to the edge of the beam.

"They are ready for you, okay?" he says and stands her next to the beam. "You are strong and brave Lexi," he whispers as he backs away, leaving her all alone standing by the side of the beam.

"Alexis?" the Judge says and raises her arm to signal she is ready for Alexis to start her routine. I am not sure if Alexis is going to salute the judge back or run off the mat and out of the arena. Finally, with an expressionless face, she salutes the judge back and turns to the beam.

"Strong, Lex!" I hear James yell and I can tell he is just glad she decided to start her routine.

Alexis stands all the way up out of her mount. She does her pose without very much confidence and then prepares for her handstand. She does a nice kick before the handstand, but when she actually kicks up into the handstand she does not go all the way up. Her feet tap together, but not over her head. She steps down cautiously and when her feet hit the beam she wobbles as she comes up into her lunge. She fights to stay on the beam and corrects herself back into the lunge.

"Way to go Lex, keep fighting," James says.

Then she does her beam dance into the arabesque and does a really solid arabesque with no wobbling. Now it's time for the leap. Alexis pauses on the beam longer than usual and we start wondering if she is going to do her leap. Just when James starts walking toward the beam, Alexis starts taking steps down the beam and James stops. She does a small leap, but bigger than the one after her crash. When her foot lands back on the beam she steps forward with a huge grin. And her grin remains in place while she does her pose, jumps, and turns. She loses the smile just before her dismount, but I know she is happy with her routine.

Her feet hit the ground out of her dismount and when she turns to the judges I have never seen her smile brighter.

James runs over to her and gives her a big hug, picking her up off the ground. "I knew you could stay up there!" he bellows, and she laughs with pure joy.

James sets her down and Alexis walks over to sit with the team while I get up and walk over to James. I high five Alexis as we pass each other.

Chapter 16

Cross Handstand on Beam

"Paige, do the routine you've been doing," he says to me. "And show off your beautiful dance, okay?"

I nod okay and he backs away so the judge can salute me. I salute back and begin my routine. I do as James says and try to do the routine I have been practicing. I stand up and do my poses before the handstand. Then I kick up into a nice and controlled handstand and come down into a solid lunge. I feel graceful and steady as I move through my routine to my arabesque. The arabesque is exactly how it should be and I easily step out of it and continue to my leap. I show off my poses and straight jumps with the shoulder and neck position Madame Julia has taught us. I make my tip toe turn and half turn with no problem and I feel great. This routine is amazing and all I have left is the dismount. I kick up into the handstand thinking about how I just rocked beam and I do my best dismount.

"Way to go, Red!" I hear James say as I salute the judge.

I walk over to James for my high five and he gives me a big hug instead. It was a good routine! "Great job!" he says, and turns me to go sit with my team.

I walk back to my seat and James turns his attention to Savannah, who is up next. My teammates give me quiet hugs since they know Savannah is about to start. She looks ready and confident waiting for the judges.

As Savannah is saluting I hear Trista whisper to me, "8.75! That's amazing, the best score so far."

"How is that possible?" I whisper back.

"Well, the whole thing was perfect. I only got a 6.8," Alexis answers.

"Really?" I say confused. I mean, her routine was a little timid and wobbly, but not that different than mine. "But we both stayed on," I say.

"Yeah, but Paige, you know I didn't get credit for a lot of the skills in the routine," Alexis answers.

"You don't seem upset," I say.

"I'm not, I'm just glad beam is over and I'm ready to have fun on the other three events," Alexis whispers.

"Good idea," I say with a grin.

"Let's watch Savannah," Trista says to us so we stop talking and watch her. She is so cute as she stands up out of her mount. PBGA's own mini-gymnast.

Savannah is very slow up there, but more steady than she usually is. She has fallen in every meet this season. I really hope she breaks that streak today.

She does a steady handstand, her best one yet. And when she finishes in a solid lunge James claps a couple of times without saying anything.

I know I'm not the only one worried about her falling because it seems like we are all holding our breath as Savannah slowly moves through her routine.

She has just finished her stretch jumps and is doing clean pivot turns.

"You've got this," I hear Trista whispering as Savannah does her half turn. All she has left is her dismount. She kicks up into her handstand and does a perfect dismount.

She gives the judges a cute dimpled grin as James walks toward her clapping, "At-a girl!" he says. She runs over to him and he picks her up in a huge hug. "I guess if you are going to stick only one routine all season, State Meet is a good meet to pick," he says laughing.

Savannah is laughing and bright eyed as he sets her down and they walk over to the rest of us.

"Great job ladies," he says to us, grinning from ear-to-ear. "Phew, I can relax now."

"But Marissa still has to go," Trista says.

"Marissa is not like you four jokers, she does exactly what she is trained to do in a meet. I don't worry about her," he says as Marissa salutes the judge.

James is right. Marissa does a routine just like she does every day in practice. We are all happy for her as she bounces over to us after her solid performance.

"Alright, let's relax and watch St. George Gymnastics compete before we start to think about floor." We watch some of them compete, but some we miss. We whisper about who came to the meet to see us.

"Did you guys see Madame Julia came to see you?" James points to the stands.

"She did? I thought she hated us," Trista says.

"She doesn't hate you guys; she actually thinks you're funny. You drive her crazy during practice, but she laughs about it after," he says.

"What is there to laugh about?" Marissa asks.

"That you guys always want to be upside down and that you are so impatient with what she is trying to teach you. She calls you monkeys," he confesses.

"That's what Trista's sister, Madison, calls us," Savannah shares.

"Gymnasts," the meet director says on the loud speaker, "that completes your first rotation, please march to your next event."

Chapter 17

Dance Pose on Floor

We line up behind Savannah and I take my place at the back of the line. I have time to think about what just happened. We just rocked beam and I have a real shot at the All-Around. We walk by our parents and they clap and wave.

"It's time for one-touch on floor. Set your stuff down and get going," James orders.

I do as he says and I line up with my team and the other two teams along the floor. A girl is standing with a timer, waiting until all the gymnasts are ready.

"PBGA, I want to see one round off back handspring and one bridge kick over and a leap. Then you're done," James announces.

"One touch begins," the girl with the timer says.

I go through the skills James tells me to do, but I feel jittery and keyed up. I can't stop thinking about the All-Around as a real possibility. If I placed I would for sure move up to Level 4 and I would be a State Champion.

"Paige, what's going on?" James asks. I shrug, not sure what he's talking about, I'm just happy and maybe a little nervous.

"Something's off, what are you thinking about?" he asks.

I'm silent. I don't want to admit I'm already day dreaming about winning this whole thing.

"Paige?" he asks and I cave.

"I'm thinking I can win the All-Around," I whisper.

He grins and says, "Oh, so your competitive spirit just showed up with that beautiful beam routine, huh?" he chuckles. "Alright, first, you can't get ahead of yourself. I want you to go get a drink and by the time you come back I want you only thinking about floor. Not winning, not losing, just doing a great floor set. Got it?"

"Yeah," I agree.

"Hustle," he says and turns back to my team. I stand and watch the other teams on floor warm up differently than us. Then I shake my head and walk toward the front of the arena where the parents are sitting. The drinking fountain is by the stands and the front door. As I make my way over to the fountain I hear my mom and dad yell my name and see my brother scramble down from their second row perch to see me. I know we're not supposed to talk to parents during a meet, but my brother doesn't understand so I decide to say hi to him.

"Hey Paige! Mom made me stop playing my DS to watch you on the bar," he says with a grin.

"Beam," I correct.

"Beam," he says. "Good job."

"Thanks, squirt."

"Did you fart?" he asks with real concern.

"No! Jason!"

"Well that's good then, at least you didn't fart real loud while you were on the bar. So that's good."

"Beam," I correct again.

"Beam," he repeats and grins.

"Okay, Jason," my mom says walking up and grabbing his hand. "You looked great up there pumpkin," my mom says. She knows we are not supposed to talk to family during a meet. So she winks at me and walks Jason back over to his seat.

At least I didn't fart, I think as I lean over the fountain and take a drink. This thought and my brother's real concern over the farting makes me smile to myself. My smile gets bigger as I walk back to floor. Jason is such a goon.

"There's a smile. You're not so serious now, that's good," James says as I walk up. "I'm going to ignore that you were talking to your parents," he whispers to me. I smile at him, surprised I got caught.

"You're after Alexis, so go sit between her and Savannah." I sit down and settle in to watch St. George Gymnastics compete.

Chapter 18

Round off Back Handspring on Floor

Now that we have been having dance lessons with Madame Julia for the last few weeks, I can see what she is talking about in the posture and dance of the other teams. The St. George Gymnastics Team can do all of their skills, but it's not very pretty. They are kind of jerky in their movements and don't really move to the music.

I lean over to Savannah and whisper to Trista, "Now are you glad we have Madame Julia?" I ask.

Trista looks at me and shrugs, "Not really, you're the only one that looks nice; I still look like that."

"Guess you're going to have to work hard to beat me," I say with a grin.

"Not really," she throws back, "I've beaten you all season; this is just another meet." I sit back and smile to myself. Trista will beat me, she's right. She has beaten me on floor all season. But I like teasing her, it seems to be how we have gotten back on track to being friends again and I like her banter. She reminds me of Alexis' brothers and how they tease each other when they are getting along really well. I never understood it before now.

Thinking of Alexis' brothers reminds me of Trista's secret. I look up to the stands and search the audience. I spot my family easily and I see that all of the PBGA families are sitting together. I find Alexis' parents one bleacher above my parents. They are sitting with all four of their boys. Three of the four boys are playing video games on hand held devices, but Drew is actually watching the meet. This makes sense as Drew is a gymnast too and is probably truly interested in watching.

I lean around Savannah's back and tap Trista on the shoulder. She looks at me and I mouth, *did you see he's here?* I ask silently. *Who?* She asks silently by shaking her head and raising her eyebrows. *Your boyfriend,* I mouth. At this she goes pale, leans forward so I am blocked by Savannah, and ignores me. Oh no, my nice little balance I found with Trista is gone. I'm not sure what to do so I just quietly watch Aerials compete on floor and hope Trista forgets about Drew.

Finally, it is our turn to compete floor and Marissa is starting us off. As usual, Marissa does the exact routine she does in practice and James is happy with her. Then Alexis is up and her routine looks better than I have ever seen it, I can tell she really tried to place her arms and head in the positions Madame Julia showed us. I stand up as Alexis finishes her routine and I make my way to the edge of the floor to wait for the judges. James finishes talking to Alexis and then walks over to me.

"How's it going, Red?" he asks.

"Fine," I answer, not knowing what else to say.

"Good. Do me a favor and show this dark little gym what a real dancer looks like. Light up the room with more than your hair," he says with a grin.

"Okay," I nod, too nervous to smile.

"Okay," he says and backs away from me. The judges are making final notes on Alexis' routine and I am forced to just stand there and wait and be nervous.

At least you didn't fart real loud, I hear my brothers voice. Oh my gosh, what if I fart? I put my hand to my stomach, it doesn't feel upset, but still it could happen.

The judge looks up and says to me, "Paige?" *Oh no, she's ready.* I salute her back and walk the few feet onto the floor to my starting position.

There's music, if I fart real loud the music should cover it up. Focus Paige, focus. Don't mess up State Meet because you're thinking about farting for heavens sakes! Think about your routine. Think

130

about dance. Chin up. I lift my chin and just then the music begins.

Feel the music, jump with pretty arms, shoulders down, show off that face!

I stop hearing my brother's voice and even my own voice and I hear Madame Julia's voice reminding me how to move. I do nice jumps and a pretty pose in the corner as my routine starts. I do a beautiful kick into my bridge kick over. I bend my knees a little in my bridge to get back over. But then I do another pretty kick into my handstand forward roll.

Next is my leap and I remember to extend my legs rather than to squeeze them and I can feel that my leap is clean and graceful. My back extension roll to push up position is okay. I stay hollow but my arms bend. I show off my face by keeping my shoulders down as I slide into my splits and rotate to my middle splits.

I enjoy the music and I can feel the beauty of floor exercise as I do the dance movements that are on the ground. I stand up and complete a clean turn and do the best round off back handspring I can. My legs come apart a little but I have a decent rebound out of it. I can hear my mom cheering as I take a knee to the ground to finish my routine. When the music ends I hold the final pose for two seconds like we have been taught and in that time I can hear James say, "That-a girl, Red!"

I stand up and salute the judge and walk over to see James. He gives me a high five and says, "And a star is born! Great job Red, way to show it off!" I grin back at him and he steers me back to sit with my team. Then he heads over to Savannah who is waiting to go next.

"Very nice," Trista says, "you may beat me after all."

"You think?" I say.

"Naw, but I like to give you hope," she answers. Then she looks at me with a solemn face and says, "Seriously, Paige, that was nice."

"Thanks. You ready?" I ask her, knowing she is up after Savannah.

"Yeah, except you made me all nervous earlier," she answers.

"I did? How?" I ask

"By bringing up you-know-who," she says.

"Who are you guys talking about?" Alexis says. And with that inquiry we both shut our mouths. How can we possibly explain to Alexis that Trista has a crush on her brother? "Are you guys okay?" Alexis asks, aware of our silence. *Think of something, fast!*

"I'm . . . just . . . nervous," Trsita says

"About floor?" Alexis asks, raising an eyebrow.

"Well, yeah, because . . . ,"

"Because Madame Julia is here," I cut in. "And Trista is nervous that if her dance is bad that Julia will be even harder on us," I lie. Oh no, I lied. To Alexis. Great. I'm turning out to be an awesome leader. A leader who lies, worries about farts, and gives away her teammates secrets.

"Oh, well," Alexis shrugs, "with season over I doubt she'll be that hard on you. You'll be fine Trista. Just do what you always do on floor." Then Alexis turns back to watch the end of Savannah's routine.

I turn to Trista and I see the relief on her face that her secret is still safe. I nod to her and she nods back and mouths, *thank you.*

The music ends and I can hear Savannah's mom going wild, "Yay, Savannah! Great job," she yells. Savannah gets up and salutes the judge with her adorable dimpled smile and blue eyes. As she skips off the floor I notice that her applause from the parents is a lot louder than the rest of us. She has captured all of them with her cute little self. Her blonde ponytail is swinging as she walks over to give James a high five. He holds his hand up above his head and she has to jump for it and the crowd loves it. Savannah seems unaware of the attention she's getting and that makes her even cuter. When she sits down the laughter from the crowd settles down as they wait for our last floor competitor.

It looks like Trista's nerves are gone as James walks over to talk to her. She is all smiles ready to do what she loves, compete floor.

"What'd you get?" Marissa asks me.

"I don't know, I forgot to look."

"How do you forget Paige? How will I know if our team is doing well or not if I don't have your score?"

"How do you know anyway? Where are you writing it down?"

"I'm just adding it up in my head," she explains.

"You're weird."

"I know," Marissa agrees unapologetic.

The floor music starts and we turn our attention to Trista. She really is fun to watch on floor. Her bridge kick over is code-of-points perfect. And her smile and pure pleasure at competing makes up for her disappearing neck on her leap. She, of course, ends with a perfect round off back handspring and a huge rebound, showing that she has enough power to do a back flip.

Trista gives the judges her winning smile and bounds off floor over to James. He high fives her and walks her over to us.

"Great job on floor ladies. Take a break and watch beam finish competing, and then we go to vault."

Chapter 19

Level 3 Vault

"Look, Paige, four scores count and there are four of you. I don't know why I need to do bars," Trista is frantically trying to convince me she doesn't need to compete on bars. We set our bags down over by vault and get ready for a quick one touch warm up.

"Trista, why are you asking me? James is the coach."

"But he said it was final and if anyone can change his mind it's you, he likes you."

"I'm not going to change his mind," I sigh. Then I turn to Trista, "Let's get through vault okay? We are the first team up this rotation so we need to focus on vault right now."

"Yeah, okay," she agrees and we line up over on the vault runway to do our quick warm up.

After we each take a turn doing one vault, James settles us in the order we are competing. Vault in Level 3 consists of running, hurdling to a spring board, and jumping to a handstand onto a stack of mats. Then falling with a straight body onto the mats. In Level 4 we will vault over the vaulting table. All of us have practiced over the table a few times so doing vault onto the mats has become easy for most of us. Except for Savannah, the mats are pretty high for her. This is the only event where her small size makes the skill harder.

Savannah is up first, then me, Trista, Alexis, and Marissa is last. Savannah is ready and waiting to salute the judges. I'm sitting at the edge of the group watching Savannah. She looks nervous. Well, she always looks nervous. But she looks extra nervous for vault today. I feel bad for her that it is so tall. The judge salutes her and when Savannah salutes back the judge gives her a winning smile.

Savannah runs, hurdles onto the spring board, and jumps into a handstand. But her handstand does not make it to a complete vertical positon, her toes don't make it over her head. Her feet come down and she falls out of the handstand into a standing position on the springboard.

This surprises all of us, including Savannah. She looks like she is not sure what to do. James walks over to her and whispers to her. She turns and salutes the judge to signal she is done with this vault. Then she walks off the spring board and is walking back down the runway with James by her side.

I'm not sure what the judges are going to do with her score. She didn't do the skill, so does that mean she gets a zero? I look at my teammates and they are quiet as they watch Savannah and James walk toward us.

"You get two vaults, so forget that one and let's try again," we hear James say. They are almost at the

end of the runway so she can start another vault. "Drive
your heels off of the board fast so you can get enough
power and speed to get the handstand over," he
instructs. I see Savannah nod and she looks terrible. A
nervous wreck.

"You can do this Savannah!" I hear myself yell.
I don't know what to do for the poor girl, I figure
cheering her on is better than nothing.

"You've got this!" I hear Trista yell.

"Focus," Marissa chimes in.

We know Savannah well, and she needs to stop
thinking about the phone in her mom's hand and think
about this vault.

Savannah salutes the judges and tries again. This
time when she hits handstand on the mats she holds it
for a second and none of us know if she is going to fall
back to the board or make it over to her back like she is
supposed to. Finally, she tucks her chin up to her chest
and this makes her fall to the correct side. She pops
up for a salute with a huge smile and the crowd goes
wild. They love her. Everyone was captivated to see if

she would make the second vault. She bounds over to James and he lifts her up in a big hug.

I stand up and walk to the vault runway. I feel so big and oafy. Savannah is a tough act to follow. And her near miss made her even more lovable. I'm so tall compared to her, and thicker, even my hair is bigger. I know she is only a second grader and I'm a fifth grader, but somehow, in this arena, none of that matters. She's a Level 3 and I'm a Level 3. She is tiny and cute and I am not.

"Paige?" I hear James coming up to me from the other end of the runway, "what's going on?"

I give him a weak smile, *what's going on?*

"Whatever is on your mind forget it and think about vault. Run fast, drive your heels, tight body. Okay?"

I nod. *Vault. Fast, heels, tight. Got it.*

He turns and trots back up the side of the runway to be over by the spring board and mats for my vault. The judges are down there too. They are so far away from me that they hold up the little green flag when they are ready for me. I salute back and step onto the runway.

I do just what James has taught me; run, punch, heels, tight handstand, fall straight to a flat back.

"That a girl!" he claps as I salute the judges and jump down from the mats. He high fives me and walks with me to the end of the runway so I can do my second vault.

"That was beautiful. On this one I want you to be straighter between the board and the handstand; try not to bend in the hips. Fast heels instead."

I nod and he gives me a quick arm squeeze and backs away, heading back up the runway to be by the mats again.

This time I'm relaxed, one vault down. There is no pressure with this second one. I salute the judges, run down the runway, do my vault as straight as I can, and when I sit up to salute the judges I can hear James again, "That's how it's done, Red!"

I'm all smiles as James walks me down the runway to sit by the rest of the team. As I get to the team he splits off to talk to Trista who is standing ready for her vault. I get high fives from the girls and quickly sit down to watch Trista.

Trista, Alexis, and Marissa all do nice vaults and before I know it our entire rotation of teams are done vaulting. I'm sitting next to Trista, since she vaulted after me, and she is watching the bar competitors closely. I'm not sure what she is looking for but her expression is intense.

"I'm worse than every girl here," she says in a low voice.

"No you're not, you just rocked three events," I point out.

"I mean on bars. Every girl I have watched so far has made all of her skills."

"We are at State Meet, of course they can do their skills," I blurt out. As soon as it is out of my mouth I know I said the wrong thing. *I am a terrible leader! What is James thinking?*

Trista is now biting her nails and has not taken her eyes off bars.

"Trista?"

"Yeah?" she says absently.

"We need you."

Chapter 20

Pull Over on Bars

"You don't need me," Trista insists for the tenth time. We're over at bars where we have completed our one touch and James is headed toward us.

"Paige, Savannah, Alexis, Marissa, and Trista," he announces and we shuffle around until we are sitting in order.

"I'm last," Trista observes. "So if everyone hits, can I still scratch?" He looks at us for a moment, Trista is, in fact, at the end of the order. Then he gives a curt nod and walks over to stand next to the coach from Aerials. I watch them chat for a minute and I can tell James is frustrated with us. With me? I couldn't get Trista to compete. That was the one thing he asked me to do today.

I watch the last girl from St. George finish her routine and I stand up and walk over to the edge of the bars to wait for the judge to be ready for me.

James walks up with his hands in his pockets. "You know what to do Paige," he says.

That's it? You know what to do? And he called me Paige instead of Red. Now I really know he's mad. *Why am I in charge of the nagging I-am-not-doing-it, you-don't-need-me Drama Queen?*

The judge salutes and I salute back without a smile.

146

I don't know what the big deal is. It's a simple routine. We don't even go up to the high bar. I'm thinking this as I do my glide and then my pull over. *Why is Trista so stubborn?*

I do my front hip circle and shoot through, except on my shoot through my foot hits the bar and I barely make it. *Dang it; that was a huge mess up. Pull it together Paige and make the rest of the routine.* I switch my grip to a front grip, lift my leg off the bar, and lean forward for my front mil circle. I make it around but I have to slap my top leg down on the bar at the very end to keep from falling backwards. This is terrible! *But you have not fallen . . . yet,* a little voice says. I quickly do my basket swing with bent legs and I swing my leg over back to a support position. I do a quick back hip circle and dismount. I do not stick the landing.

I turn and give the judge a weak smile and walk over to James. He has a serious expression but still puts his hand out for a high five.

"What happened?" he asks.

"I'm not sure," I shrug.

"What were you thinking about?" he presses.

I can't answer him so I just shrug and look down. I wasn't thinking about my routine. I was angry. Angry I couldn't get Trista to compete. And now I've blown it. I have no chance to get a medal in the All-Around. A gymnast has to hit every event to have a shot at the All-Around medal. My lack of concentration let that shot slip through my fingers.

James knows this too. He puts his arm around my shoulders and silently walks me over to my team.

"A good meet Paige, but it won't be enough to place in the All-Around," he says.

"I know," I nod, looking straight forward. My eyes are stinging and I don't want to look at him right now.

"Great. You were supposed to hit!" Trista says when James and I walk up to the team.

"You know Trista, sometimes it's not always about you!" I fire back at her, much louder than I expected to. The girls from St. George and Aerials have all turned their heads and are looking at us. Okay, I didn't mean to be so loud, but Trista is seriously under my skin!

James grabs my arm to keep me from sitting back down, "You two, come with me," he says to Trista and me.

Trista looks shocked as she stands up. I'm not sure if she is shocked by my outburst or James' orders to come with him.

We follow him to the wall at the edge of the gym, slightly away from bars. "Now, I don't have all day, Savannah is about to start," he says impatiently. "You two stay here and work it out. You decide together if Trista is going to compete. This meet, this sport, this day, is for you. Not me. If you place, it's for you, not me. I'm done caring more than you do. I'm going back over to bars. Figure it out and come back and tell me what you have decided." He turns away from us and hustles back over to bars just as Savannah is saluting the judge.

We look at each other, shocked. We made him mad now, he rarely gets angry.

We stand there silent for a minute. Then Trista speaks, "Look, I'm sorry. I know it's not always about me. I'm just really bummed you flubbed."

"I didn't flub."

"Yeah, you did," she says with agony in her voice. "You were supposed to hit so I could just sit back and not do bars today."

"What's the big deal, Trista? So you do bars, and you might fall. So what? All of us have fallen this season. We all make mistakes."

"But I told you why!" She leans against the wall and slides down along her back until she plops down on the floor.

"You really are such a Drama Queen," I say, and the moment the words are out I slap my hand over my mouth.

Her head snaps up, "What?"

"Oh come on, it fits you perfect, it was going to come out sooner or later," I say, taking a seat next to her.

"I don't think it fits that well," she sulks.

"Trista, do you really think Drew will like you less if you mess up?"

"Yes! He's so good at bars! He can do kips and giants on the strap bar and he might laugh at me."

"Well, would you laugh at him if he fell at a meet during floor exercise?"

"No," she answers quickly.

"Why do you like him?" I ask.

"Because he likes gymnastics, and he's nice to us and his sister, and he's cute. Really cute," she answers.

"He *is* cute," I agree with a smile. "If you wouldn't laugh at him for messing up, he probably won't laugh at you for messing up," I say. I'm not sure if this is true, but it seems reasonable to me. I don't really know much about boys. I only know that 5-year-old boys are obsessed with farting jokes. "Besides, you don't really want a dumb boy to keep you from doing things you like to do, do you?"

"If he's that cute I do," she sasses back.

"Trista, we have to go back over there. What do you want to do?"

"I don't know," she groans.

"Look, I flubbed. I lost my shot at the All-Around. And we are about to lose our chance at a team placement if you don't compete. I really want to place as a team. Don't you?" I ask.

She doesn't say anything. She's not arguing with me so I guess that means she is considering doing her bar routine. I stand up and grab her hand to help her up.

"You just want a flub sister. I can't believe Savannah gave up my secret name. I'm going to kill her," she grumbles as we start to walk back over to bars.

"Don't be too mad at her, we kind of guessed it," I say.

"You guessed? How is that possible?" she asks as we stop at the edge of the mats to wait for Marissa to finish her routine. "Don't answer that," she says, which makes me giggle.

When Marissa dismounts we cross the bar mats to be with our team.

James sees us and asks, "What will it be?"

"It looks like I'm up," Trista says.

Chapter 21

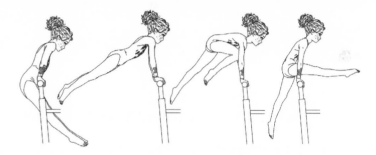

Shoot Through on Bars

James stands with Trista to speak to her before her routine while I go over and sit down with my teammates. "How did you guys do?" I ask.

"We did fine, but it was lonely competing without you two here," Alexis answers.

"Sorry," I say as I sit. And I really am sorry I missed seeing their routines.

"Is Trista really going to do it?" Marissa asks.

"I think so," I say with a grin.

We watch as James backs away from Trista so she can be ready for the judge. The judge salutes her and Trista salutes back, and surprisingly, there is a smile on her face.

She begins her routine with a perfect glide and pull over. Then she pauses before the front hip circle. She bends her knees to make the front hip circle around, but the completion of the skill has her smiling. Then she casts as high as she can and makes her shoot through. This is followed by another grin. She's doing it! And making it!

Trista changes her grip and lifts up her front leg and hips for her mil circle. This is the skill that she has never made in practice. I grab Marissa's hand and hold my breath.

"You've got this!" Savannah yells.

We are all nervous for her.

But that little Drama Queen swings around and makes her mil circle like she does it every day. Savannah jumps up and starts clapping and the rest of us join in. Trista easily makes her basket swing, back hip circle, and swing down. She takes a little step on the landing and turns to salute the judges. Her smile lights up the entire arena and I can tell she has surprised herself with that routine.

James runs over and gives her a hug and we are right behind him. We crowd around the two of them in one big group hug.

"Ladies, ladies, over here," James says pulling us away from the bars so St. George can compete. "We are going to stay over here until the rest of the competitors are done. Then you can go see your parents, okay?" We nod in agreement.

James gives us a huge smile, "Great job today ladies. I think we may have upset some of the bigger teams."

"Really?" Trista says.

"Yes, we had four solid routines on each event. It will be interesting to see how it plays out. For now, all we can do is sit and wait."

"James?" I say.

"Yeah?"

"What were my scores? I didn't really see any of them, except for beam," I admit.

James chuckles, "Red, I don't know many competitors that completely miss seeing their own scores," he says.

"Well, I didn't really see anyone's score," I admit.

"Stay here, I'll go see if I can get the print outs," he says and walks over to the head table.

"You are such a dork, Paige, how do you miss seeing scores?" Trista teases.

"Well, I was dealing with your drama all morning," I shoot back and she give me her big grin.

"I think you got a 7-something on bars," Marissa tries.

"Have you guys been watching the Salt Lake Gymnastics Team?" Alexis asks. "They're on beam, look at them, they're perfect."

"That must be what Julia wants us to look like," Marissa points out.

We sit there in awe of the girl on beam and when she finishes we silently watch the next one who looks just as beautiful.

"Wow," Savannah breathes. "Did you see how long she held her handstand?" she asks. We saw, we haven't torn our eyes away from beam.

"Their entire rotation is just them," I observe.

"Why aren't some of those girls in Level 4?" Trista asks.

"Good question," James says as he walks back up. "Some of them may not be old enough for Level 4, but most of them should be in Level 4."

"Well, that's not fair," Trista squeaks.

"Nope, it's not. But this is gymnastics, not track, I never promised you fair," he says completely unconcerned about the injustices of gymnastics. "I have your score cards, well, sheets in this case," he says and hands us each a piece of paper.

"Very nice meet ladies," he says as he hands me my paper.

My paper looks like this:

Utah State Championships – Region 1

Team: Perfect Balance Gymnastics Academy

Competitor: Paige Green

Age group: 8-10

Vault: 7.90

Bars: 7.35

Beam: 8.75

Floor: 9.05

All Around: 32.80

How did I score so high on floor? This score card doesn't seem right. I look up at James, "I don't think this is right," I say.

He steps closer to me to look over my shoulder, "What's wrong with it?" he asks.

"Well, I know beam is right because I saw that score, but the rest seem wrong." I say.

"They look right to me," he says, "I saw all your scores come up."

"But how did I score so high on floor when my back handspring is so hard for me?"

"You had a clean routine. A slight leg bend on your back handspring and bridge kick over is about it. It was beautiful, with nice dance and solid skills. Your score is right," he confirms.

I stare down at the paper in my hand. And here I thought vault and bars were my best events. But beam and floor surprised me today.

"Paige your improvements on dance and your willingness to learn what Julia was teaching these last few weeks is what has made the difference for you today," James explains. He pats me on the shoulder and I give him a smile.

Cleaning up my dance made my All-Around score a full point higher than in past meets. I'm glad Julia was here today to see that we did learn something from her after all.

"Alright, that was the last competitor on beam. You girls can go see your parents and come back to the floor when the meet director announces awards."

Chapter 22

Sharing the Podium

"Great job today pumpkin!" my mom says as I climb over the first bleacher to get to my family.

"Thanks."

"How do you think you guys did?"

"As a team?"

"Yes, as a team. How does it work?"

"Well, five girls compete and four scores count," I answer.

"It's lucky you had five girls then," my mom says. Then she frowns, "how does it work for a team like that? Do they take the best five scores from all of them?" my mom asks pointing to Salt Lake Gymnastics.

Hearing this question, Alexis' mom leans forward, "I can answer that for you," she says. "Each team has to designate five girls to represent them. Since they have about 20 girls, they probably created three or four teams."

"Three or four teams?" my mom says.

"Usually what teams like that do is pick their best five and call it the A team, then the next best five is their B team, and so on."

"How do you know all this?" my mom asks.

"Oh, I did gymnastics growing up and in college," Alexis' mom explains.

My mom and Alexis' mom keep talking about how scoring works while we put our warm-up pants and jacket on. I see teams gathering on the floor and so I zip up my jacket and head back to the floor too. The meet director has dragged out the awards stand that has a spot for 1st through 6th place.

I sit down near the 6th place spot and know my team will be joining me soon. Not a second goes by before Trista comes running up and plops down next to me.

"Drew said he liked my routine and he called me scrappy," she says with a huge grin.

"You are scrappy, aren't you?" I say grinning back.

"Thanks for making me do it Paige. It was so fun and I can't wait to compete again," she says.

And that's when I know that I did it. I really am a leader. I encouraged Trista to compete bars and she did it and she's glad. I made a difference for her, for the team today. And it feels great.

"I'm sad the season is over," she continues with a pout.

"I know, I can't believe it's over either," I say.

"What's over?" Savannah asks as she sits down with us.

"The season," I say.

"I know," she agrees, "but now we get to work Level 4 stuff at practice."

Alexis and Marissa join us as the meet director gets on the microphone. She thanks us for a great day of State level competition. Then explains that she is going to start awards with individual events, then All-Around, then team scores.

"We are going out to tenth place on each award but we are going to start with first place so that the first place girls have longer on the podium. We will do that for all of the awards except for the team awards."

And with that she begins with vault, announcing the winners and handing out medals.

Marissa got 6th and Alexis placed 4th. Everyone else on the podium was from Salt Lake Gymnastics. Savannah got 5th on bars and Marissa got 8th. I'm busy looking at Marissa's medal when I hear, "In 7th place, Paige Green."

I scramble up from where we are sitting and go stand on the 7th place spot next to the podium. A volunteer comes up and loops a medal over my head while they announce 8th, 9th, and 10th place.

"These are your Level 3 State Beam Champions. Ladies, salute!" We all put our arms up in a salute and the parents quickly take pictures. Then we know to all get down and go back to our teammates.

As I'm walking back to my spot on the floor the meet director begins announcing the floor exercise winners. Just as I sit down I hear, "Paige Green and Trista Thompson."

"What is it for?" I ask Trista.

"You guys tied second on floor!" Savannah says excitedly.

"We tied?" I say, surprised, I didn't know we got the same score.

Trista jumps up, "Guess you have to beat me another day," she says and we walk up to share the number two spot on the podium.

And oh, it is so fun up there! We get to stand up and wait for the other places to be announced. I look down at my medals. One silver and one bronze. This silver one is the coolest. Third place through tenth are all bronze, and of course first place is gold, but the fake gold almost looks bronze. I like the silver the best.

I flip it over and I see it has a sticky label that says, Paige Green, floor 9.05, 2nd place, Utah State Level 3 Championships. Then I look over at Trista, she is grinning from ear-to-ear. I lean into her for a little shove and she looks at me. "This is better than beating you," I say.

"Yeah, I'm surprised I don't mind sharing," she says with her usual spunk.

"Ladies and gentlemen, your Level 3 State Floor Champions, salute!"

Trista and I salute, smile for the cameras, and jump down from the podium and go back to sit with our team.

We watch as Marissa gets eighth place in the All-Around and Savannah gets tenth. For the All-Around, Savannah and Marissa get a small trophy that has a gymnast on the top doing a handstand. Marissa lets me look at her trophy as she sits back down. It says *Level 3 State All-Around Champion Eighth Place.*

"Wow, you guys that is so cool," I say with envy. I'm disappointed I didn't place in the All-Around. But it felt good to help my team and I'm not as sad as I thought I would be. Maybe next time I can do both.

"And now to your team awards. We will start with Tenth Place this time. In tenth place, Salt Lake Gymnastics C Team," she says.

"Holy cow, their C Team placed. Those are their worst girls." Alexis points out.

"Shh, Alexis!" Marissa says

"They can't hear me," she says.

"In ninth place, St. George Gymnastics," we clap for our friends from St. George. They looked the same as us, so now I'm not sure if we placed. Well, maybe they had more falls, I can't remember.

"In eighth place Flips B Team." Five girls from Flips stand up and head to the podium, leaving the rest of their team on the floor, which I find kind of sad.

"In seventh place, Aerials Gymnastics." Again, we clap for the girls we briefly made friends with. Now I am convinced we did not get anything.

Marissa leans over to me. "There is still Flips A team, Salt Lake A and B, doesn't leave many spots left for us to place."

"I thought you added it up. What was our score? She has been giving scores," I point out.

"I didn't see all the final score sheets. James wouldn't let me," she explains.

"In sixth place, Logan City Gymnastics."

"In fifth place Flips A team."

"In fourth place Park City Snow Bunnies Gymnastics."

And then we hear it, "In third place, Perfect Balance Gymnastics Academy."

We did it! We made it to the podium! We all jump up and squish onto the third place spot as a lady comes over and hands us a trophy. She gives it to Savannah, who is standing in front of all of us. We can hear our parents going wild and taking tons of pictures. We smile proudly as the meet director continues.

"In second place Salt Lake Gymnastics B team."

"I am pretty sure we know who won," Trista whispers to me.

"And your Level 3 State Champions . . . Salt Lake Gymnastics A Team!"

We stand on the podium as Salt Lake Gymnastics cheers and celebrates and makes their way to top of the stand and the five of them cram onto a first place spot made for one person.

"That concludes your Level 3 Utah State Championships," the meet director says. "Join us back here in two hours for the Level 4 State Championships."

We all jump down and people go everywhere. All of a sudden the meet is over, music comes on and parents are on the floor taking extra pictures of their kids with the medals and trophies

"Paige?" I hear and I look down. It's Savannah, "What do I do with this?" she says holding out the team trophy.

"Give it to James," I say with a grin. "Better yet, to James and Julia," I say.

"Well, where are they?" she asks looking around.

Just then James walks up, "Great job today ladies. I knew that with all those hit routines you guys secured a team placement. But I didn't expect third! Way to go," he says grinning.

"Oh honey, I'm so glad you're still holding that!" Savannah's mom exclaims, let's get you up on the first place spot with that trophy for a picture.

"But I didn't get first and this is the team trophy," Savannah says.

"Oh, just for fun honey. Jump up when this girl gets down," her mom instructs.

Savannah does as her mom says and climbs to the top of the podium and smiles for a picture with the team trophy. It really does look like she won the entire meet up there standing above the "1" with a big trophy in her hand.

"How did we pull it off?" I ask James as our team disperses to talk with family.

"That final bit of dance and polish was our secret weapon," he says patting me on the back.

"Oh, is Julia still here?" I ask him. He nods and points to where she is talking to some parents. "Stay here," I say to James and run off to get Julia

"Excuse me," I interrupt her.

"Yes, my little principal," Julia says.

"What's that?" I ask.

"It's a ballet joke. The top ballerina in a show is called the principal dancer," she explains.

"Oh. Thanks," I say a little embarrassed she thinks I am the top. Although the group she is comparing me to are not exactly into dancing.

"Did you decide if you are a gymnast or a dancer?" she asks me.

"I'm both," I answer with a grin, "I learned that I can be both."

"I was hoping you would say that," she says putting her hand on my shoulder. "I think all the best gymnasts are both," she says.

"Can you come with me for a team picture?" I ask.

Julia gives me a huge smile and follows me to the podium for the chaos of picture taking.

"Wait with Savannah and James," I say as I run to go get my mom and other teammates.

"Mom!" I yell as I see her through the crowd.

"Oh, there you are pumpkin. You ready to go?" she asks.

"Not quite; can you come over and take a picture for me?" I ask.

"Sure," she says, "Jason, stay with Daddy, I'll be back," she instructs. Not that it was necessary, he's playing his Nintendo DS and won't move until she makes him.

"I have to round up the rest of the team. Will you wait with Savannah and James?" I ask.

"Sure, but do you want me to help you? Marissa is about out the door," she points out.

"Yes!" I yell, "go get her," and I trot off to get Alexis and Trista.

I find Alexis and Trista talking with Carmen, who came with her parents to see what a gymnastics meet is like. "Sorry to interrupt, but I need these two for a picture."

"Oh, can I take it? I love taking pictures," Carmen says. I nod and the four of us head back to the awards podium.

Finally, I have our team together. "Savannah, will you and Alexis sit on the first place spot?" I ask. "Then I need you two to stand in front of them," I say to Alexis and Marissa. They nod and stand in front of Savannah and Alexis. "And Julia, I need you here," I say having her stand to the left of us, and James you here," I say pointing next to Julia. Since I am taller than the other girls if I stand in the middle between Trista and Marissa I will block Savannah and Alexis. So I kneel in front of where Trista and Marissa are standing.

With all of my gathering and arranging, all of the PBGA parents and Carmen are ready with cameras. We smile and they all start taking pictures like crazy. As I'm smiling for the picture, front and center, I finally do feel a part of this group. Even better, I feel like their leader. It's fun to be the oldest one after all. I'm able to help James and my teammates.

"Are we done yet? My cheeks hurt," Marissa says.

"Almost," I say, and I stand up and turn to Savannah. "May I take this?" I ask Savannah, gesturing toward the team trophy. Savannah is surprised by this, but she hands it to me. I walk over and hand it to James and Julia.

"Thank you both," I say. With that my teammates clap and shout their thanks to James and Julia.

"Oh, I think this belongs to James," Julia says refusing to take the trophy I'm holding out for them.

"I'd like you to both hold it for one more round of pictures," I explain.

"After all," I add, "dance is the secret event."

Up Next?

Alexis' Story

Book 4 in the Perfect Balance Gymnastics Series

Boys Have Talent Too

Chapter 1

"Alexis, what is this flier?" my mom asks holding up

a blue paper that says Winter Wonderland Talent Show.

"It's a talent show," I say.

"Are you going to do it?" she asks, her blue eyes

sparkling with delight.

I decide to mess with her a little. "Maybe. I'm not sure. What would I do?"

She puts down the paper and starts rummaging through my brothers' back packs. "Well, I know what I would do if I were you, Baby Girl," she says pulling out more papers and skimming them.

My mom calls me Baby Girl because I'm her fifth child and only girl. She says she will always call me her baby. I don't really mind. And I've noticed that since I started third grade she stopped calling me Baby Girl in public.

"Boys!" she yells upstairs, "Table time!" A thunder of boys come running down the stairs.

"How come she's not at table time?" Ethan asks, as he passes me at the kitchen counter.

"She's still finishing her snack. She eats like a lady, unlike you oafs," my mom teases.

I pick up my apple slice and slowly eat while I listen to my mom settle the boys at the table. Table time in our house is when we all sit at the dining room table and do homework. We don't eat at the dining table all week because it's a huge mess of books, homework, papers, pencils, crayons, backpacks, and glue. But on Sunday my mom clears it off so we can have a family dinner after church.

I have four brothers, Josh, William, Ethan and Andrew. My oldest brother, Josh, is at basketball practice and the rest are with my mom in the dining room.

"Andrew, when is this book report due?" I hear my mom exclaim.

"Friday, I think," my brother responds.

"Good thing you've been reading Adeline Falling Star, you can use that," she decides.

I hear groaning from Drew that he has to finish the book Mom has been making him read.

"Alexis! You should be done by now. No more stalling," my mom shouts to me from the other room. The trouble with being the youngest is that my mom knows all the tricks. I bet Josh never got rushed during his after school snack when he was a third grader.

I jump down from the stool and walk into the dining room. William, Ethen, and Drew are bent over their homework. My mom has my spot all ready with my spelling words out.

"Let's see, when are try outs?" My mom asks picking up the blue paper again from a pile she has brought in from the kitchen.

"For what?" Drew asks looking up.

"There's a talent show at Mountain View. You should do it too," my mom says to Drew.

"What would I have to do?" Drew asks.

"Some tumbling to music," my mom says. Drew is my only brother that is not into basketball or baseball. He does gymnastics, like me.

"No thanks, boys don't tumble to music," he informs her.

"In talent shows they do," she says.

"Alexis can do it," he says, and goes back to his homework.

"Do you want to do it Baby Girl? I would help you put something together," my mom says. I can tell she really wants me to do the talent show.

I was excited about it when my teacher explained it to us in class. But I thought Drew would do it with me.

He can tumble so well, it would be so cool if we both did the show. I glance up at my mom and she is waiting for an answer.

"Not by myself," I confess. "Are you sure you don't want to do it, Drew?" I ask my brother. He looks up and shakes his head no.

"Male gymnasts don't perform to music," he insists.

"Maybe my teammates will do it with me?"

"What a great idea," my mom exclaims, "you can ask them at practice today."

"Can they come over on Saturday? To make something up?" I ask, getting excited about the idea. Paige could create the dance and Trista could do her back flip. Everyone at school would see how cool it is to be a gymnast.

"You have the PBGA Team Banquet and sleep over this Friday. Why don't you just make up something at the sleepover?" My mom asks.

"The banquet is this Friday?" I ask. "Finally," I add.

"I know it feels like you've been waiting forever, but is only January and your season ended in November. December is a hard month to do anything.

I'm sure Katie and James were just busy. Anyway, better late than never." My mom says, walking over to her spot at table time. She sits down and picks up her book to read while we work.

"Will we get trophies like the boys do after baseball and basketball season?" I ask.

"I'm not sure, probably not. My guess is each of you will be recognized in some way. But gymnastics isn't really a sport that gives participation trophies. Maybe because you get medals and ribbons all season."

"What do you mean recognized in some way?" Drew asks.

"When I was a kid Most Improved and MVP got trophies. But Katie tends to do things differently, so I'm not sure. We have to just wait and see," she says looking down at her book.

"What's MVP?" I ask.

"Most Valuable Player, dork. Haven't you been to all the same baseball banquets I've been to?" Drew asks.

"Yeah, but I never paid attention; they're boring."

"Hey!" Ethan looks up from his work, "It's not as if a gymnastics meet is a picnic. The same stupid music over and over again, it's a nightmare!"

"At least no one is spitting!" I yell.

"Hey, you two," my mom raises her voice and we immediately stop shouting. We don't want to be in here longer than we have to. She has extra workbooks and worksheets for us to do if we misbehave. We quiet down and go back to our homework.

I stare at my spelling words while I think about the banquet. Would I be MVP? No, probably Marissa. Most Improved then? That would probably go to Trista. Did I do anything special this season? What about Paige and Savannah? What would James give them? I hope we all get trophies.

After we all get trophies we can go to the sleepover and make up the best gymnastics and dance routine ever. And we will perform it at my school and all the kids will think I am the coolest kid to ever go to Mountain View.

"Alexis," I look up and my mom is staring at me, "are you ready for me to give you a spelling test?" she asks.

"Yes," I say. It's lucky that I'm good at spelling. She'll think I was studying instead of day dreaming about trophies and talent shows.

To learn about other books written by Melisa Torres go

to **melisatorres.com**

For Perfect Balance Gymnastics Series updates

go to **facebook.com/pbgseries**

Read all the books in

the Perfect Balance Gymnastics Series!

About the Author

Melisa grew up in San Jose, California where she trained at Almaden Valley Gymnastics Club for ten years. She then went to compete for Utah State University where she was a two-time Academic All-American and team captain.

Melisa stays involved with gymnastics by substitute coaching and choreographing floor routines. Gymnastics taught Melisa fitness for life. She stays fit by weight lifting and ballroom dancing.

Melisa is a single mother to two active boys. Their favorite things to do together are skiing, swimming, going to the library, and dancing in the kitchen.

Made in the USA
Middletown, DE
28 January 2019